You Could Be That Kind of Girl

STORIES

Téa Franco

word west press | brooklyn, ny

isbn: 979-8-9893940-6-7

published by word west in brooklyn, ny

first us edition 2024

printed in the usa

www.wordwest.co

cover & interior design: word west

Table of Contents

I. Soft-Spot Kisses

Creation Myth of a Mixed Girl.................................... 7
Sunday Bloom...9
Bevy... 19
Carlos... 31
They Call Us The Girls... 39
5 Methods of Coming Out to Your Parents..................... 45
Frida Returns..51
Polycystic Ovary Syndrome Reimagined.......................... 59

II. How to Become Enough

Up Next: I Dye My Hair Blonde.................................65
The Comfort of It... 69
Becoming Beyoncé in Three Easy Steps!....................... 79
You Could Be That Kind of Girl.............................. 83
Fiona Apple Joins Our Crochet Club........................... 93
Loose Blood... 99
A Raccoon Died at Fountain Park............................. 113

III. Someone Better

Everyone Likes Taylor Swift.................................... 119
Tent City..123
Apparition of the Virgin Mary in the McDonald's Drive Thru........ 137
Peanut Butter... 149
Where Do Skunks Go When they Die?........................... 163
The Spottiest Leaves.. 179

I.
Soft-Spot Kisses

Creation Myth of a Mixed Girl

Before Salomé's grandmother bought the polka-dot cookie jar she often let Salomé dip her hands into, before wrapping the scraggly scarf finger-knitted by Salomé around her neck, before doling out suffocating hugs and soft-spot kisses, before braiding her heavy hair with arthritic fingers, and well before she met Salomé—three months after she was born to a father whose skin was three shades too dark, hospital-pink faded from her baby cheeks—you'd never guess Grandmother tried to run over Father with her rusted Corolla.

This was before Father was Father and Salomé's mother was Mother. This was after Not-Yet-Grandmother caught Not-Yet-Mother sneaking back into her bedroom window after meeting up with Hopefully-Never-Father to split a slushy in the 7-11 parking lot, cherry-stained lips, deciding they'd give Salomé an accented name, even if it was hard for Some-Day-Grandmother to pronounce.

After Not-Yet-Grandmother told Not-Yet-Mother she couldn't date Hopefully-Never-Father, after Soon-To-Be-Mother's stomach showed her secret, Soon-To-Be-Grandmother dragged her along while she tailed Soon-To-Be-Father in her car. After Soon-To-Be-Grandmother followed Soon-To-Be-Father home, after Soon-To-Be-Father got out of his car and waved a hesitant hand, Soon-To-Be-Grandmother slammed the gas as Soon-To-Be-Mother screamed and held her stomach where Salomé stirred, unaware that if Soon-To-Be-Father hadn't spent his life saving himself from a world that wants him gone, then Thankfully-Now-Father may never have felt Salomé's squishy fingers wrap around his thumb.

Sunday Bloom

Aleda found the first ladybug in a pocket of the hand-me-down pants her older sister Bria wore in second grade. Aleda thought the jeans—wide-legged with orange zipper pockets—were the coolest. Her mom found them while going through boxes in the basement, but when Aleda put them on, the zipper wouldn't budge. Her mom looked up at her daughter, head down and jeans unzipped, and flipped through the remaining clothes.

"You've gotta lay off the snacks," she said, pulling out a larger pair. "We can't afford new pants."

The bigger pair of jeans had holes in the knees and grass stains on the butt pocket. As Aleda peeled the zippered jeans off her body, a small ladybug crawled out of the front pocket. She put out her pinky and it crawled on, looking up at her like it wanted something.

"That's a sign of good luck," her mom said as she closed the bin and pulled herself up off the floor. "But get it out of the house."

Aleda brought the bug outside and tilted her finger to the pavement, creating a bridge the ladybug didn't walk. She puffed air at it, but its pinprick legs sunk deeper into her skin. At dinner, the ladybug crawled on her feet and when a piece of rice fell from her fork, the ladybug sucked up her mess like a self-driving vacuum cleaner. And it went on like that, the ladybug searching for food and Aleda obliging. He followed her to school where he ate her lunches and never saved any fruit snacks for her. So, naturally, she named him Welch.

***

"Has your mother been forgetting to feed you? Or can you just not stomach all the gringa cooking?" Tía Sonya laughs to herself while pinning parts of Aleda's handmade First Communion dress, preparing to take it in again three months after Welch showed up. Aleda traces a pinky over her collarbone, holding back a smile as Sonya zips up the dress, fabric sagging around her belly.

Aleda barely eats her mom's food. Instead, she feeds it to the bloom of ladybugs following her around. Welch wasn't big enough to make a dent in her food, but each week more ladybugs arrive in larger groups looking for bits and pieces from Aleda.

After pinning the dress, Sonya hands Aleda the clothes she arrived in: a Girl Scout camp sweatshirt and the perfectly-fitting zipper jeans. Sonya hangs up the dress and leads her niece to the kitchen, where Tío Juan is cooking dinner.

Aleda's mouth waters at the kitchen's bright, savory scents of plates heaping with rice, chicken,

10

and tostones. Her stomach flips as she realizes she will have to feed all of this to her bloom, who gets cross with her if she eats too much.

She sits at the table and eats her meal in small nibbles, sneaking scoops of rice into her pocket when Juan and Sonya aren't looking. She fits some of the chicken in her too big hand-me-down sneakers, but she eats the tostones because there is nowhere to hide them.

Aleda offers to clean the kitchen, so Juan and Sonya will leave the room long enough for her to go outside and feed the bloom. When she steps out the back door, they emerge from beneath rocks, holes in the wooden fence, and inside the grill—a colorful infestation on the dull patio.

Her ladybugs came from all over the place, traveling from other countries after word traveled of a little girl who liked to feed bugs. As the bloom grew to its current size of 112 ladybugs, she spent hours searching through articles online to learn more about her bug friends: yellow and black ones from Asia and North Africa, orange ones from Europe, gray ladybugs from who-knows-where (all she knows is they bite when they're hungry), metallic blue ladybugs from New Zealand who glimmer in the dark as they sit on Aleda's bedroom windowsill at night, and brownish ladybugs from Puerto Rico who came home in her backpack when she visited her great grandmother during Christmas break.

Aleda empties her pockets of rice, dropping the grains to the ground, and laying the chicken beside it where the ladybugs—who she had taken weeks to train into being polite and orderly—take turns slurping it up.

As her first Communion approaches, the bloom gets hungrier. With so many new bugs, Aleda begins mixing them up, but she always recognizes Welch as the leader of the pack. With 187 ladybugs now in the group, they claim her entire breakfast and lunch, but dinner isn't the same as she eats under the watchful eye of her mother.

"I gave you enough spaghetti, there's no need to get more," Aleda's mom says, making sure Aleda doesn't get seconds, which is good because the less food she is given, the easier it is to sneak it to the ladybugs. But still, Aleda must eat at least some of her food in front of her mother, which makes the ladybugs angry. Every night after dinner, the gray ladybug bites her toes while she sleeps, which keeps her awake in fits about how much she'd eaten.

On the morning of her first Communion, Aleda's mom helps her zip up her still-too-big dress. The lace sleeves and high neckline tickle Aleda's skin, but she likes what she sees in the mirror and her mom seems to approve as well.

Bria came home from college this weekend to help Aleda do her hair and makeup. As she puts glitter eyeshadow on Aleda's veiny eyelids, Aleda feels Bria's sharp breath before she puts a hand on her cheek. Aleda hears Bria whispering to their mom later, asking if Aleda is sick, but their mom just keeps telling Bria her sister looks perfect.

Aleda isn't allowed to eat or drink or pee while wearing her dress. She sits on her bed with Bria until it is time to go to the church. Aleda feels a tickle on her foot and looks down to see Welch crawling up her frilly white sock.

"Those things aren't as lucky as Mom makes them out to be," Bria says, reaching down to swat him away. Aleda moves her foot out of Bria's path and smiles at Welch as he nestles his speckled body in the tulle.

Thirty minutes before the service, Aleda's mom drops her off at the front of the church, kisses her goodbye, and lets her walk into the giant wooden doors alone. The next time her mom sees her, Aleda will be a new person. Or at least she thinks that's what's supposed to happen. She's not always good at paying attention during CCD, especially not recently.

Walking into the church, Aleda feels small under the vaulted ceilings. She sits with her classmates, who can't sit still for longer than ten seconds. It's like they all have ladybugs crawling in their socks. She decides maybe some of them could, too.

She sits at the end of the pew with her head in her hand, not feeling up to fooling around with her friends. She focuses hard on breathing, hard on staying awake. Her feet dangle off the pew, not quite touching the emerald-green carpet below.

It starts off like a normal Mass, hard to sit through in a dress twice as poofy as Aleda's usual Sunday Mass dress. She feels more ladybugs crawl into her socks. After kneeling and standing and praying and trying her best to sing along to hymns even though singing winds her now, it is time for the Eucharist. With thirty ladybugs hiding in her socks, She and her classmates line up, white cupcakes about to receive their first Communion. The stained-glass windows reflect red, blue, and green glints of light, dancing around the communicants as they approach the altar.

When it's Aleda's turn to receive the Eucharist, her legs are tired of standing. She replays the steps in her head, because even though she doesn't know what would happen if she messed this up, she imagines it's bad. Like going to Hell bad. Before the priest puts the wafer on her tongue, she gets nervous to eat it, realizing she should've given it to the bloom. The ladybugs on her ankles rile when she puts it in her mouth, scurrying up her legs and biting her when she swallows it.

At the end of Mass, they drive home and Aleda's mom has her change into her party outfit, a pink satin dress with little roses on the collar and sleeves hanging loose around her arms. Their guests arrive soon after Aleda finishes getting changed.

It's mostly family, but some kids from CCD who aren't having parties of their own are there too. It's one of the first warm weeks of the year, so they hold the party in their backyard. Her parents even splurged for a bounce house designed like a church, with an inflatable cross on the front. Aleda steps into the backyard soaking in the sight of so many people there for her and listening to the covers of her favorite music played by Bria's old high school band. There are white tables lined with tons of food, and Aleda breathes in the scent of it, the ladybugs dancing in her socks, biting her ankles in anticipation of what's to come.

Before the party gets too crowded, she makes the bugs in her socks join the rest of the bloom— consisting of 208 ladybugs—in the shed, where because she is sick of them tickling her ankles.

Aleda rejoins the party where aunts and uncles she barely remembers the names of pinch her cheeks and hand her thick white envelopes. Bria's band soundtracks the younger cousins as they run in circles, yelling after each other as they glide into the bounce house, where they fling themselves around in a chorus of yelps. Aleda watches her cousins jump around red-cheeked when Chris and Gemma from her CCD class call her over to the snack table, where they are filling their plates with chips and dip.

"Come eat with us!" Gemma says. Aleda knows there's no way to sneak food out to the bloom with so many people around, which means she shouldn't eat and wait to feed them until the party ends. But she is hungry. And she wants chips more than anything. And she thinks maybe people who have received their first Communions need to eat to be strong enough to serve God. She picks up a paper plate, filling it with food.

The three new communicants eat together, Aleda chewing on carrots, and then chips, and then drinking juice. She forgot how good food can be. Her bloom will be mad at her, but there will be plenty of leftovers.

After they eat, her friends run towards the bounce house and Aleda follows. For the first time in a while, she feels strong. She can run and jump like her friends. She is weightless and alive as she watches her friends fly around her, as she feels laughter bubble in her gut—it makes her want to be better.

When her parents announce it's time for cake, Aleda is dragged down to Earth. Her dad opens the box containing the three-tier white cake with gold crosses on it. He lets Aleda cut the first piece, urging her to cut a big one, and she plops it onto the plate, ready to hand it to someone else, but her dad pushes it towards her.

"This is too big," she says to him.

"It's your big day, so it's your big piece of cake." Aleda's mom frowns at the large piece, but doesn't say anything about it in front of the guests.

"You won't be able to eat so much when you're my age," Aunt Karen, her mom's sister, says, squeezing her shoulder and laughing. Aleda sits down and her friends join her a few moments later.

"You're lucky you got a big piece," Chris says. Aleda eats her cake in little bites, knowing she can't get away with sneaking it to the ladybugs when everyone watched her cut it, since everyone had something to say about it. She takes bigger bites without thinking. She feels a pinch on her calf and looks down to see the grey ladybug on her leg. She flicks him away.

As she eats more of the cake, more ladybugs appear on her leg, Welch at the lead. She doesn't want to share. She's been hungry for a long time. She brushes the bugs off her legs and stabs bigger forkful of cake into her mouth. The gray ladybug crawls back up her leg, leaving bites along her calf. She swats at the bugs some more.

"What's on your leg?" Chris asks as she squirms and flinches. Six ladybugs fly up around her head, flying towards her friend's plates, trying to steal their food. Gemma swats at the bugs, and more fly out of the shed to join them. Soon all of them are out, a rainbow wave terrorizing her party guests and eating their cake.

The music is drowned out by the screams of people running and bumping into one another, knocking others into the ground—leaving grass stains on their knees and cuts along their arms—to get into their cars and leave. The band stops playing when they see the swarm.

Aleda's parents try to calm the guests, but shrieks escape their throats as they swat the bugs with rolled up placemats. Some of the adults who didn't make it out in the rush join her parents, hitting the ladybugs with whatever hard object they find. Aleda watches the ladybugs get smashed into tables, watches their guts splatter onto rolled up placemats, leaving behind black sludge. Bria runs into the house and grabs a can of spray the family uses to kill palmetto bugs in the summer months and begins spraying it into the air. Aleda watches the ladybugs she had been caring for fall to the ground, watches their corpses crushed by fleeing feet.

Aleda doesn't want to hurt her friends. As her family murders dozens of members of the bloom, She tries to warn the bugs. She tells them it's not safe here, they need to leave, she will feed them later, but the bugs don't listen. The bugs only want to eat everything they can get their mouths onto, with no regard for the consequences. Aleda knows it's her fault the bugs are getting killed.

All she can do is watch her family destroy her bloom. She thinks of all the work she did to take care of them, only to lose them after one meal. She wished she'd had more control, she wished she hadn't wanted cake so badly.

After the swarm dies down and the adults give up on killing them, only thirty ladybugs remain. They go back into the shed and hide in the darkest corner, eating a piece of cake Aleda managed to save for them in the mess.

After helping her parents clean the disaster, Aleda climbs into the bounce house and lays there, staring at the inflatable ceiling, as it wriggles from the moving air within it. She feels the soft rubber under her body and her crinkled dress pressed into her skin. Outside, the sky swirls deep blues and purples as her father, not realizing his daughter is inside, begins to deflate the bounce house. She lays there, flat and unmoving as it deflates around her, her body lowering towards the ground, creating an indent in the shrinking rubber. As the final air is sucked from the structure, Aleda feels Welch crawl back up her leg.

Bevy

Martina sat alone in the corner of her bedroom, braiding bright threads into friendship bracelets. In her lap sat 100 strangely named colors, from macaroni & cheese to outer space. Ariel gave her the thread, after announcing to their parents that she—a soon to be middle schooler—was too old to play with string.

As she decided if her next bracelet would be traffic cone and cotton candy or starshine and robin's egg, the screen door clicked open. Martina leaped and ran, socked feet silent on the carpet.

"Mom said I can come with you to Ellie's house."

"We don't want to hang out with you." Ariel slipped her feet into blue sneakers.

"I'm coming or else I'm gonna tell mom you left me home by myself."

"Whatever," Ariel said, sighing so hard her curly bangs shuffled.

Martina skipped down the street behind Ariel, imaging what it would be like to have a best friend.

Martina used to have a best friend, but she moved all the way to Georgia and left Martina alone, left to follow around Ellie and Ariel even though they didn't want her there. They used to tolerate Martina when they were still in the fifth grade, but after their graduation, things changed.

Ellie was out front, tossing a basketball into a lopsided, rusty hoop at the top of the driveway. She was wearing a pair of pink running shorts Martina recognized as being hand-me-downs from her cousin. They didn't fit Ariel, so their mom gave them to Ellie.

Ellie passed Martina the ball and she lunged for it, the ball slipping past her grip and bouncing off her toes.

"Martina, I didn't know you were coming," she walked towards the rolling basketball. "We can play hide and seek instead."

"You have to be it first though," Ariel said. Martina hated being it, but she would do it if she got to play with her sister. She placed her hands tight over her eyes and began to count aloud.

"One mississippi two mississippi three mississippi four mississippi five mississippi sixmississippisevenmississippieightmississippi TEN." Martina prowled the yard for them, deciding which of their favorite hiding spots she'd hit first.

Under the porch, she nearly stuck her pink sneakers in an ant pile. In the garage, she lifted each of the rusty tools Ellie's mom used to fix the neighborhood cars for extra cash, as if her sister would be hiding behind a wrench. She climbed up the rickety ladder of the squat treehouse Ellie's dad built her before he left a year ago, but instead of finding them she found stacks of baseball cards Ellie collected.

Martina wasn't allowed to touch these. She hovered over the piles, stretching her fingers towards them and looking over her shoulders. A rustle in the trees. Ellie? Just a squirrel. She was alone, so she spent some time on the floor of the treehouse, leafing through the water spotted cards, deciding she didn't understand the big deal about them. As she ambled down the treehouse ladder, she thought she heard a shuffle of feet near the house. She jumped from the last rung of the ladder and ran towards the noise.

Shed? No. Picnic table? Maybe. She walked back to the porch and lifted the tablecloth, spotting only a family of worms. A giggle shattered the silence of the yard. The porch door slammed shut. Martina whipped around, she had them.

Hiding inside was cheating—but Martina would let it slide this time. She crept up to the sliding door and pulled, but it wouldn't budge. She peered through the glass, the sun's glare making it hard to see. Martina tiptoe-teetered until she saw two heads of brown hair poking up from the couch. The heads were shaking in laughter, and the *High School Musical* TV series played on the television.

"Let me in!" Martina pounded her fist on the glass door, leaving a smudge of dirt behind. One of the brown-haired heads rose from the couch.

"Go home, loser."

Martina blinked, leaned closer to the glass.

There Ellie stood, fingers to her forehead in the shape of an L. Martina turned around and ran off the porch, nearly tripping. Her cheeks were red and wet. She couldn't let them see.

The sun burned bright in her eyes as she walked home, cheeks glistening with rejection. Mr. Roberts was mowing his lawn, filling her nostrils with the wet smell of grass. She kept her eyes on her toes as she passed, making sure the notorious tattle-tale didn't see her sniveling. The last thing she needed was for her mom to remind her she was too sensitive.

Her feet quickened and she saw her house in the distance, moments aways from hiding in her room to read. On the sidewalk, she spotted something strange: a big, black circle deep and dark enough to swallow her whole. She stopped and squinted at it. She looked around, worried it was vandals, worried they were nearby. Martina was afraid of the big, tall teenagers who lived in the neighborhood. They walked down the street at night, followed by the clink clink clink of the cans they dropped in their path. Those teenagers were bad, and they were mean. They liked to scare people, but after one incident where they chucked cans at her, they left Martina alone because they feared her dad who—large and strong from his days toiling away at the auto shop—looked much scarier than he was.

When she was sure the boys weren't nearby, she took careful steps towards the black hole. As she braced herself to be sucked in, she noticed fiery orange veins sprouting through the circle. Another step made her realize it wasn't flat. Was it a rock?

Another step. She reached out, placed a hand on top. It was cool and slick. The rock moved, and a head popped out.

Martina jumped back a bit. A turtle? She gazed past the creature, towards the lake her dad liked to fish in. Did he live there? She looked at his tiny head. His eyes were sad. She tried to pick him up, but he popped out his legs and scuttled from her grip. Martina had always heard turtles were slow. This turtle must have been special.

"You wait right there, buddy." She ran into the garage, filling a large bucket full of water, soaking herself in the process. Heavy now, she dragged it back. The turtle had waited there, just for her. She tried leading him into the bucket of water, but he was as stubborn as Ariel. When she finally managed to pick him up and put him into the bucket, she thought she heard the turtle sigh with relief.

Martina dragged the bucket into the kitchen, heaving it onto a chair. She opened the refrigerator and peered in, wondering what turtles eat. She pulled out a GoGurt and examined it. He wouldn't know how to slurp the yogurt from its plastic tube. She put it back. She scanned the contents of the fridge and settled on lettuce, pulling a head from the back of the vegetable drawer, removing one leaf. She replaced the head in the fridge, placing the side with the missing chunk towards the back.

The turtled inhaled the lettuce like Martina ate limber de coco bought from the old lady down the road, giving herself a brain freeze. She dragged the turtle up the stairs to her room, hiding the bucket in her closet. She looked at him, floating. He traveled very far from home.

"I should give you a name." Martina could have sworn he nodded his head at her. Her head filled with power as she filtered through names, deciding on Camilo, after her favorite character in the movie *Encanto*. Camilo would need a better home. Martina found an old wagon in the shed and cleared out space on her closet floor for it, before filling it with water. As she placed Camilo in his new home, she heard her parents walk into the house, keys jangling. She slammed the closet door and ran downstairs.

"You tracked dirt in," her mom said. Martina shuffled to the closet without protest, grabbing the broom and sweeping up the mess while her parents put up the groceries and then sat on the couch, watching *Law & Order* at full volume. Martina tried to sit with them, but they shooed her away, so she went outside to collect rocks and twigs. While she was filling the pockets of her denim shorts with outdoor treasures, Ariel returned.

"You totally lost at hide and seek," she laughed, looking down at Martina who was crouched over a pile of dirt.

"I don't care. I found a better friend after I left Ellie's stupid house."

Ariel kicked over the dirt pile with her sneaker and ran inside, Martina following. In the house, Ariel grabbed the last freeze pop and, without asking, their dad cut the top open for her. Martina looked in the freezer, hoping there was something else for her, but there was only frozen chicken and ice.

"Did you girls have fun today?" their mom asked Ariel.

"Loads of it," she answered, her mouth full of hot pink ice and juice dribbling down her chin. Martina slipped out of the kitchen, rejoining Camilo in the closet, where she read him a book. He swam up close to the edge of the wagon and popped his head out to listen to Martina's words.

The next morning, Martina woke up first to steal more lettuce for Camilo. After he ate, Martina laid in bed and read until she heard her parents stirring in the kitchen. Her dad was making pancakes and her mom was nursing a cup of coffee. Ariel was sitting at the table telling her parents about a dream she had the night before. In the dream, she was best friends with Olivia Rodrigo.

Her dad finished making three pancakes and gave them to Ariel. He turned off the burner and sat down. Her mom slid him a cup of coffee.

"Papi, can I have pancakes?" Martina asked. Her dad looked startled to see her there.

"Why don't you make yourself some frozen waffles?"

"Girls, how about we go to the zoo today?" Martina's mom said between sips.

"I guess that could be fun," Ariel said. Martina could tell she was trying to act cool because her hand was twitching the way it always did when she was excited for something.

Martina remembered Camilo needed more water. She shoveled waffles into her mouth so she'd have enough time to give him some before they left.

"When are we going to get home?" Martina asked.

"What, do you have somewhere to be?" her dad joked. She laughed and ran upstairs before anybody could ask more questions.

"I am going to be gone for a while to go to the zoo. I'll see some of your friends there," she said to Camilo. He blinked at her from inside of the wagon. After saying her goodbye, Martina went downstairs, slipped on her crocs, and waited to leave.

At the zoo, Martina saw the peacocks from what felt like miles away. Their bright blue wings were on display, and they looked proud. She walked towards them, almost in a trance, ignoring the other animals nearby. She stared up at the birds, and all the colors on their wings reminded her of the colors of threads for her friendship bracelets, all the ones she had made so far stacked onto her thin wrists. The peacock's wings were colored with ocean wave, tart lime, and squashed berry.

Martina loved reading the informational plaques at the zoo and headed straight to the sign next to the enclosure, where she read that a family of peacocks is called a bevy—which her dad called their family after Martina told him what she'd read. She watched the male's colorful wings unfurl, all of them moving in groups. The plaque said this is how they prefer to live, avoiding isolation. They did better when they had company.

When she finished reading, her family had moved on to the giraffe enclosure. She jogged to catch up, making it in time to watch the zookeeper feed the giraffe a banana. Ariel gasped at how its long purple tongue spiraled around the fruit before pulling it into its mouth. When they approached the aquatic animals, the world was tinted blue from the water surrounding them. Martina stood there, nose nearly touching the glass as sharks and anemones puffed by. She saw a group of sea turtles, dancing across the water.

After the zoo, her parents left the girls at home while they went to buy groceries for dinner. As soon as their car pulled out of the driveway Ariel went to Ellie's. Martina didn't bother asking to join. She had a plan. Once she was alone, Martina put on her swimsuit and pulled Camilo down to the lake. At the shore, she stripped off the big t-shirt she was wearing and removed Camilo from the wagon, walking them both down the shore and into the water.

As the water iced her skin, Camilo squirmed. His legs and tail shifted as he tried wriggling out of Martina's hands. She tightened her grip and continued into the water until her feet couldn't touch the bottom, pumping her legs to keep herself afloat. As she began to feel balanced, her legs in a repetitive state and Camilo resting comfortably in her arms, he bit her hard, and Martina startled, letting him go. Now freed, he swam far and fast, keeping just out of Martina's reach.

Martina cried, tears and lake water colluding to make it harder for her to see as she attempted to swim towards her friend. Her legs tingled and she opened her mouth wide to catch more air, but instead sucked in water as Camilo got further away, pumping his tiny turtle legs until he was just a small, black hole ahead of her.

Martina and her now rubber legs had gone further out into the lake than she intended. Weary and sad, she tried to swim back, but with each pump of her legs she slipped under instead of moving forward. She flailed her arms, trying to force her body above water, but the water was wrapping itself around her ankles, pulling. She opened her mouth in a scream, but water filled her throat only allowing a gurgle to escape. The water filled her ears. Her eyes. She was scared. Inhaled more water. Couldn't see. Wanted to scream. There were hands on her wrists. They pulled up instead of down.

The mysterious hands belonged to an old man in a fisherman's hat. He pulled her into his boat, where his wife wrapped a towel around Martina's shoulders. The strangers sat there in silence, slowly rowing to shore while Martina cried. When they approached the dock, the old women helped Martina keep her balance as they exited.

"Sweetie, what's your parents' number? We need to call them," she said, pulling out a black flip phone sealed in a plastic sandwich bag. Martina's parents would be angry if they found out where she was.

"You could've really gotten hurt today, them letting you go out here all by yourself," the man said. Martina looked around. She knew where she was. Without thinking, she ran towards her house. The old lady's towel flew off Martina's shoulders. They

called out to her, but she kept running, every few
moments looking over her shoulder, seeing if they
would follow.

Carlos

A Better Life Rehabilitation Center was committed to the full recovery of their patients; the forefront of this commitment was isolating addicts from their friends and family. Celia thought this was bullshit. But their mom was dedicated to A Better Life's promise and wouldn't let anyone visit Carlos, even on his twenty-seventh birthday.

Instead, they sat at the table a week before to make him cards. Celia volunteered to take the cards to the post office. She went in and bought three stamps, but instead of handing the woman working the desk the envelopes, she took the stamps back to her car and stuck them to the envelopes herself. She didn't want anyone knowing where her brother was.

***

Carlos' face was lit up from the flames of eighteen blue candles. Celia picked blue candles because she knew it was his favorite color. His girlfriend, Julie, sat next to Carlos, the light of her phone screen illuminating her frown in the dark room. He tried to hold her hand, but Julie pulled it away.

Their mom brought out the cake, topped with eighteen striped candles and crooked words. Celia had insisted on decorating the cake because she was nine years old. Old enough to do important tasks. Carlos' attention turned away from Julie.

"Cece, did you decorate this?"

"Yup, all by myself," she said.

He nudged Julie on the shoulder and pointed at the cake. She forced a smile at Celia, giving a gentle thumbs up.

"Make a wish, Carlos!" Celia said and watched as Julie went back to texting.

***

On Celia's eighth birthday, Carlos and Julie took her to see *Frozen on Ice*. Carlos thought Olaf was funny and couldn't hold his laughter inside of himself while watching the snowman's heavy body swirl around. Julie and Celia shared an Icee out of a cup shaped like Elsa's head, making it look like they were eating her brain. After the show, Julie got a stranger to take a photo of the three of them. Celia kept the photo tucked inside her favorite book on her bookshelf. In it, Carlos and Julie had their arms wrapped around Celia who stood in the middle, cheeks pink from the cold.

***

That year the cake was smaller than usual because Julie didn't come to the party. There was just enough room for nineteen candles. Celia heard Carlos say something about Julie being a bitch, which she thought was a mean thing to say. She heard their mom on the phone a few days earlier talking about how Carlos lost her to his vices. She knew he was probably mad because a couple of weeks ago when they were in a fight, Julie threw Carlos's phone across the room and the screen shattered so bad it looked like all his texts and photos would seep through the cracks.

***

It was Celia's idea to use trick candles the next year. On her birthday one year, Carlos shoved cake in her face, leaving her light brown cheeks stained with Care Bear pink for days. It was her turn to get back at him.

She could barely sit still when her mom called Carlos downstairs. It was a moment before he made it to the table, sunken eyes looking around at his family's smiling faces. He flashed an empty smile at Celia and sat at the head of the table.

"Make a wish," she whispered, because if she said it any louder, she would have laughed.

He leaned over and blew out the candles once. The flames died down and Carlos looked ready to leave the table when the flames flickered back to life. He squinted and blew again. Each time the flames pushed itself back up to the surface.

"Are you fucking kidding me?" Carlos got up and left, ignoring the pained look from their mother. He slammed the front door on the way out.

Celia's dad filled a small bowl with water and placed the trick candles in. The bright flames

33

seeped into the water and disappeared. The party ended before it began, leaving her parents to clean up a fruitless mess, and as her mother went to put the four plates back into the cabinet, she bumped into him. Celia's dad snatched the plates from her hand.

Her mom left the kitchen, gesturing for Celia to do the same. Celia went up to Carlos's room and fell asleep in his bed, holding her sloth stuffed animal Carlos bought her last time they went to the zoo.

***

The chocolate frosted cake sat abandoned on the warped wooden table as Carlos's mom tried calling him. The twenty-one candles poking out of the top looked lifeless. Three hours later when Carlos stumbled through the door, Celia—still awake because her parents forgot to enforce her 9 o'clock bedtime—ran to greet him. He looked at Celia, smiled, then stumbled over her pink Converse she forgot to put away when she got home from school, landing face down on the ground.

He lifted his head and threw up, yellow vomit covering the floor, and laid his head back down. She shook his elbow.

"Celia, come here," said their mom, witnessing the scene from the top of the stairs.

She heard her mom call 9-1-1 and heard her dad talking to the people who came in the ambulance before they all left the house. Celia tried to follow them outside, but they closed the door on her, leaving her to spend the night in the house alone.

***

At Celia's first swim meet with the middle school

34

swim team, her parents and Carlos sat on the cold benches in the natatorium holding signs with Celia's face plastered on it. It was the first time she had seen Carlos in a few days, and his face looked bright. Throughout the meet, the signs got soaked and ink bled down the signs onto their arms, but they still chanted her name, loud enough for her to hear beneath the surface. When she finished in second place and pulled herself out of the pool, the first thing she saw was her family, covered in ink from the elbows up, running to hug her.

***

Two months before Carlos' birthday, Celia started saving up all her babysitting money to buy Carlos' gift. She cut a slit in the top of a shoe box, decorated it with purple paint, and filled it with the cash she earned from watching the neighbor's baby. On the morning of Carlos' birthday, her mom would take her to buy him the newest Call of Duty game he wanted.

On the day of Carlos' birthday, Celia was up earlier than her mom. She got dressed and went into her secret hiding place behind her bookshelf and pulled out the box. She opened the box and saw she was short fifty dollars. She began taking all the books off her bookshelf looking for a glint of green. She hoped the money had just fallen out of the box, and she would find it jammed between some of her books. She started removing the books faster, practically throwing them to the ground, ruining the perfect alphabetical order she kept them in, until the shelf was empty, and the money was still nowhere to be found.

Carlos came over before his mom was able to light the twenty-two candles on the cake. He sat down with droopy eyes. His mom tried talking to him, but he barely responded with more than a grunt.

"Carlos, I was going to get you a video game for your birthday, but I lost the money. I'm sorry," Celia said.

Carlos avoided looking at Celia when he said, "You have to be more responsible with your money, Cece." He slurred his words as he spoke, his eyes hardly open.

***

Celia's mom was in line at the Publix bakery to buy a cake. She held her phone to her left ear and in her right hand she held a package of candles in the shape of the number twenty-three, as an officer told her Carlos had been arrested for having drugs in his car.

***

Celia had a folder on her computer filled with photos of floofy ball gowns she started collecting when she was nine years old. Her perfect quinceañera dress was pink and tiered and filled with intricate beading. Her best friend Jeremy would be her escort and she would invite her entire class.

Slowly, her parents cut the budget for her party. When they had to pay Carlos' ambulance bill, she was told she could only invite a few friends to the party. When they had to start sending Carlos money for the commissary it became a family-only event. When Carlos' public defender was too overwhelmed to do his due diligence causing their parents to hire a lawyer instead, she couldn't get a dress. On the day that was supposed to be her party, Celia watched *Twilight* with Jeremy in her basement, eating sheet cake and avoiding calling her brother.

***

Celia went to the grocery store with her mom and wandered down the baking aisle. She looked at a pack of twenty-four birthday candles. She wondered if Carlos was celebrating his birthday in prison.

***

Celia laid in her bed listening to music so loud the sound dribbled out of her headphones and filled her room. Earlier, Celia asked her parents for permission to go to the movies with Jeremy, his boyfriend, and a boy from chemistry class Celia had a crush on, but her dad insisted on chaperoning. Ever since Carlos got arrested, Celia's mom repeated the phrase, "it's not you we don't trust, it's the world." Since she was seventeen and rarely thought about the world unrelated to her, she didn't believe it was the world's fault that Carlos turned out the way he did.

The album ended and she fell asleep in the cool silence of her bedroom, not noticing her parents leaving the house. Hours later she was stirred awake by a light tapping on her door. She was tempted to ignore it, but her parents rarely came to her room, so their quiet knuckle-tap worried her awake. She slunk to the door and opened it, silently inviting her parents inside. Carlos was in the prison infirmary.

37

He had tried to hurt himself. They found him alone in his cell, hardly breathing.

***

Celia stood on the diving block, toes gripping the edge of the platform, chlorine stinging her nostrils, listening to the buzzing crowd at the Southeastern Youth Swim Invitational. Her goggles gave her a tinted view of the parents, some holding signs with their child's name on it, others holding large bottles of Gatorade to give to their panting child after the race, but the goggles didn't stop her from seeing that her parents still weren't there. Carlos had a pre-trial hearing today—exactly one week before his twenty-third birthday—but her parents told her they might make it back in time.

The buzzer vibrated the natatorium, and Celia dove into the water. Her limbs cooled as she made her way across the pool. She pumped her arms and legs and hardly noticed when her hand hit the wall, coming up from the water only a second before hitting her head, and seeing she won first place. Her team ran to the end of the pool, screaming and waving, and Celia pulled herself out. She couldn't tell anyone. She went to the locker room and sat alone, waiting for a call from her parents, who had told her they might make it back in time.

They Call Us
'The Girls'

When Marisol sprained her ankle while trying out for the softball team, we all ended up with wrapped ankles. We're not triplets, but sometimes we feel each other's pain.

It became more apparent when Marisol started sixth grade, leaving the rest of us behind in elementary school. Marisol started doing things without us or without telling our parents, like trying out for the softball team even though we aren't very good at sports. When Marisol fell and sprained her ankle, we all rolled over in pain, getting sent to the principal's office for acting out in class.

We're not triplets, but everyone thinks we are. We're not triplets, but we're all a year apart. Our two younger brothers are far enough apart in age to not be mistaken.

When we get home from school we form a production line in the kitchen, putting dinner together. After everyone eats, we clean. Marisol cleans the table, Maya cleans the dishes, and Maria sweeps the floors.

We're not triplets but our dad built us a three-tier trundle bed inside the pantry. After dinner we retreat to our makeshift room, crowding around our tablet and watching *Minecraft* streams until it's time for bed.

We wake up for school while it's still dark outside. Our hair sprouts up from our heads in several directions and we all somehow swapped blankets in the middle of the night. We brush our teeth with our shared toothbrush, a red one from the dollar store with T.G. marked on the end in silver marker. We do each other's hair, rubbing in curl cream our mom buys in eight-pound tubs from Costco.

We tiptoe into our parents' room where our dresser is nestled in the corner, and grab outfits for the day: three white short-sleeved blouses and three pink corduroy skirts. The clothes are getting tight on Marisol. While she tries to button the skirt, we all hold in our stomachs and stretch towards the ceiling. When we've inhaled all the air out of the room, Marisol rips off the skirt and kicks it aside. She goes into her backpack and pulls out a gray t-shirt and blue jeans with rips up one leg. We raise our eyebrows at her.

"My friend gave it to me," she says out loud for some reason, even though we almost never use words to communicate. We keep our eyebrows raised.

"None of this fits anymore," she says, throwing

the blouse on the floor with the skirt.

Each morning, our dad drops us off at school, and each morning he almost forgets to drop Marisol off at the middle school. Each morning, we yell at him to take the turn. We say goodbye to Marisol and then we are dropped off with our brothers at the elementary school down the road. Our teachers all think we—Maria and Maya—are twins and we always want to correct them and tell them about Marisol, tell them we are triplets because sometimes we forget that's not true either.

During lunch, we are called down to the principal's office.

"You girls are in so much trouble," our mom says when we arrive. Next to her is Marisol, holding a wad of bloody tissues to her nose. We follow our mom out to the car while she mumbles about how she can't believe her sweet little girls would deface their own bodies.

"What did we do?" we ask Marisol. We all look at each other. Mom passes us tissues. We all hold tissues to our bloody noses.

It turns out a friend of Marisol's—a girl named Lia—pierced her nose in the girl's bathroom using a needle from a sewing kit she kept in her purse. Apparently, Lia and Marisol have been inseparable, but we hadn't heard of her until now. Mom says the silver stud better be gone by the morning.

The next morning, we wake up and we all have silver studs and bruises on our left nostrils. We keep the left side of our face out of mom's sight. We try to take them out but when we do, Marisol howls.

Our noses really hurt.

We stay in the pantry watching *Minecraft* until Mom forces us out. She tells us today we are no longer going to school, and she will teach us instead so she can keep an eye on us. Mom can't remember what grade we are in, so she teaches us third grade math. When we finish our worksheets in ten minutes, she accuses us of cheating. She sends us to the pantry.

As we head for the pantry, she notices our noses and demands we go to the bathroom and remove the studs. We stand lined up in the mirror and pull them out. The small fake diamonds are encrusted with our blood. We're not triplets, but we all have matching holes in our noses.

We go back downstairs, and mom shows us multiplication tables for three more hours and then makes us read until it is time for dinner. In the living room, we all huddle around one copy of *There Was an Old Lady Who Swallowed a Fly* until it's time to make dinner, a giant vat of rice and beans. Maya is the slowest reader out of the three of us, so we spend time lingering on pages, waiting. Marisol keeps trying to skip ahead, but we remind her we work together, always.

Before we finish reading, there's a knock on the window. Outside stands a girl in plaid pants. Lia. Marisol waves at her, grinning.

"Cover for me," she says, once again out loud. We've never covered for each other because we always do everything together. Marisol can sense our hesitation. "Please," she says. We go to the pantry and play on the iPad, figuring mom won't come looking for us for a while. Marisol sneaks out with Lia and comes back an hour later, red cheeked with leaves stuck in her hair. We are light and airy. We help her remove the leaves before dinner.

At dinner Mom informs us we aren't allowed to use our iPad for the next two weeks because of our "reckless behavior" and Dad puts it on a high shelf. When our parents go to bed, we try standing on each other's shoulders to reach it, but one of us is ticklish and we all giggle and fall over before we can ever get close to reaching the iPad.

After dinner we watch *Modern Family* with Dad and think about all the streams we are missing. When we go to brush our teeth before bed, Marisol tries to put the stud back in her nose but the holes are already closed. Marisol's tears run down our cheeks.

In the middle of the night, something pulls us from sleep. Marisol isn't in her bed. We check under the covers to make sure she isn't hidden. We walk around the house calling her name. We don't discuss our plan. We head out the front door, opening it incrementally so the rusted bolts won't reveal us to our sleeping parents. Our bare feet pad down the street, the moon and the half-burnt-out streetlights illuminate the way. We expect to feel her.

We walk so far we no longer recognize the houses we pass. We squint in the dark. We call for Marisol, our unanswered voice rises around us. The further from home we stray, the less streetlights there are. The stars poke holes in the black night, and we squint harder. We trip on the same cracks in the sidewalk, we jump at the same time as a skunk scurries past our toes, and we feel ourselves getting tired.

We pass a small park we've never seen before and sit down on a bench. We feel empty, just the two of us.

We aren't triplets, but we don't work when there's not three of us.

We fall asleep on the bench, leaning against each other, snoring lightly. We sleep through the night and well into the next morning, getting toasted by the sun. We are shaken awake by our parents.

"My babies, my girls!" Mom hugs us, her tears falling onto our backs. Dad joins in on the hug, feeling awkward and clunky wrapped around the three of us. "You scared us half to death," Mom says. They lead us back to the car.

"We have to find Marisol," we say.

"It's so good to have the girls back," Mom says again, starting the car and driving home with just the two of us.

5 Methods of Coming Out to Your Parents

Method #1:

Get a girlfriend with a gender-neutral name (i.e.: Jordan, Riley, Devyn, Sam or Jamie). Next, call your parents and report you are finally in a relationship. Their prayers have been answered. You will not be a lonely spinster—rejoice! Prepare for questions about his major and his family. Answer them honestly—except when they ask if he's Catholic—but instead of telling them you met her in biology class tell them you met each other in biology class. This allows you to have plausible deniability.

Then, months into your relationship and them hearing about how great it's going, your parents inevitably invite Jordan/Riley/Devin/Sam/Jamie over for a dinner of steak and potatoes, which they make any time someone new comes into the house, someone who might not enjoy their usual pasteles or pernil. Bring Jordan/Riley/Devin/Sam/Jamie back home with you and walk straight to the kitchen where your mom is cutting up potatoes and your dad is seasoning the steak. When your mom realizes Jordan/Riley/Devin/Sam/Jamie is not who she was expecting, she almost cuts her hand by mistake. Introduce her as your girlfriend for the first time.

Method #2:

Send a text to your family group chat, normally used for bragging about personal achievements—your sister's promotion at the salon where she works or your dad passing his master technician certification—or asking each other to pick up more sofrito at the grocery store, or to make Thanksgiving plans. The last text in it was about you making the Dean's list last semester. Your sister sent the eye roll emoji. Your mom sent the heart emoji. Your dad asked you who Dean is. Ignore his question and start a new text. Keep it simple: 'im gay.'

Mute the group message on your phone.

Method #3:

Call your mom while she's at work, wrangling kindergarteners into lunch lines, too busy to notice your call. Call your dad while he's rolled under a car, tinkering away at leaking pipes, his phone safely tucked away in his own car, far away from the grease and machined edges of a mechanic's life. When you are hundreds of miles away at school, leave a voicemail on their phone telling them you can't keep lying to them. That you hope they understand. That it's not their fault. Ignore them when they try to call you and talk about it.

Method #4:

Come out after Mass. Not after the service where Father Alvarez reminds everyone being gay is a sin and reads aloud from Leviticus, the passage that, when you were thirteen and kept staring at the red-haired girl in your art class, you highlighted and read every night before bed. The passage you whispered to yourself in high school when your best friend tried to kiss you and even though you wanted to kiss her back, you pushed her away. No, wait until the Mass where they talk about how God created everyone perfectly in his image. Remind them about what Pope Francis said. Remind them how much they love Pope Francis, how they whooped when the white smoke billowed from the Sistine Chapel, and they announced the newest servant of Christ. The first Hispanic pope.

"Such a gentle man," your mom had said.

Method #5:

"So, Emma and I adopted a chihuahua together.

And who knows, in the future if this really works out and she really is the right person for me, maybe we will adopt kids or something."

Say this quickly, so they can't interrupt you, and when the whole sentence tumbles out of your mouth take a forkful of rice. Scoop another. Fill your cheeks full of warm food and silence.

Your sister will continue to eat. Your dad will look at your mom who will be, as always, the first to respond.

"Are you telling us you're gay?" She'll say this in a tone you have only ever heard her use when your sister was caught drinking with her friends in the backseat of her SUV when she was sixteen. Your sister cried, but you must keep it together. Nod. Eat more rice. Your dad will remain quiet.

"How did you meet?" your sister will ask. Tell her later. For now, you're silent.

"Are you sure it's not just a phase? You never were rebellious as a teenager, maybe you're making up for it now." Your mom will get up, walk into the living room and come back with the green leather-bound Bible, a constant presence on your coffee table and in your life. She will try to hand it to you. Pick up your glass and take a long gulp of water instead. She will put the Bible down beside you.

"Why didn't you tell us before," your dad will finally join in.

"She's trying to break our hearts," your mom will say. Smooth out your napkin. Rearrange your cutlery. Don't try to explain what is.

"You guys are acting like real jerks," your sister will say.

"She has to realize what she's doing is wrong," your mom will crumple her napkin in her hands. She will keep wringing it until tiny particles fall to the table like snow.

"We want grandkids, ones who look like us. Ones we can love," your dad will say.

Let the rising voices of your parents float around you. Finish your dinner, cleaning your plate in the way that used to make your parents proud when you were a kid, even though it doesn't matter now.

Frida Returns

"I hope the exit is joyful and I hope I never return."
— Frida Kahlo

It doesn't take Frida Kahlo long to figure out how to work Instagram. She doesn't know how she ended up back in Detroit sixty-seven years after her death, with a knot in her back, a dress tinted gray with dirt, and reeking breath. On her first day in a city where she had once lost so much, she looks at herself in the full-length mirror of a room she does not recognize, tracing her hands over her body, the metal brace on her back, feeling her slender wrists and the hair on her arms. Ribbons of dead skin flake

51

off her sharp cheekbones, emphasizing the pallor spread across her brown face. She stretches her arms towards the ceiling, trying to shed decades of death.

But despite the memories dredged up by this city in a country she hates, she enjoys Instagram. Each day she stands in front of the mirror, stretching from floor to ceiling, in a bedroom she supposes is now hers and poses: a perfectly popped knee, a well-placed head tilt, and no filter, she takes a selfie.

In this life, she learns how she can take photos in portrait mode rather than painting portraits. She takes selfies so crisp you can see each individual unibrow hair and she smiles and captions the photo #hairywomenclub. She plays with filters meant to abstract her features and adds color to them.

In the first few days of her new life, she spends hours scrolling through photos of girls' selfies—young women she sees her old self in. These women have neon colored hair, sparkly eyelids, and tiny tops exposing their midriff. Frida had long ago figured out the power behind painting only her good side, and she sees these girls have learned the same.

Every time she sees a selfie of a girl glowing with confidence—Frida favors the ones with soft bodies, big hair, and spotted skin—she follows her. Often, they will follow her back, liking her selfies and paying her compliments in the comments; sparkling heart emojis and "loving this outfit" fill her inbox, causing her phone to chime all day long. People start telling her how much she looks like Frida Kahlo, so she makes her Instagram handle @notfridakahlo.

She looks at the Frida Kahlo tag on Instagram

and learns her face is on t-shirts, plastered on the sides of buildings, even on prints framed in gaudy houses she is sure belong to capitalists. She learns white women dress up as her for Halloween and a musician made a song based on the title of her painting *What the Water Gave Me*, because she thought it was cool.

Frida decides to use Instagram to fix her posthumous image. She gains hundreds of followers a day and starts getting messages about brand deals and calls from the local news station of people wanting to interview her.

The first brand deal she accepts is with Revlon, who tells her upon the real Frida's death, her husband, Diego, had kept several of her belongings including the Revlon makeup Frida always wore. They want her to recreate what they refer to as "Frida's iconic red lip" and post it to Instagram.

Frida pretends not to know Diego was wrong, pretends not to know what he shared with the world wasn't her makeup but the makeup of one of his mistresses.' She isn't a fan of Revlon, but she takes the deal anyway. She captions the photo with facts about "the real Frida's" penchant for protests and revolution. Thirty minutes later, Revlon asks her to take the post down.

Frida loses two hundred followers after another Instagram influencer @StarbucksAndTheSecondAmendment posts an infographic about @notfridakahlo claiming she is "destroying Frida Kahlo's image by forcibly politicizing her." Frida begins receiving even more messages, most of them telling her to delete her account, to stop pretending to be like Frida Kahlo, or vague threats on her life. But, Frida continues on the app, fueled by a band of teenagers who defend her, and ask her questions about her most radical stances.

The next week a fan messages her about a protest in Detroit. An annual march for women's rights. Frida remembers when she would protest alongside Diego, but was always forced into the background, posing for paintings by him and other radical male muralists who pretended to include the women while really having complete control.

Frida knows she needs to be a part of this, but also knows with the state of her back and leg and being generally out of practice moving and existing, she will need a wheelchair to use during the march. She scours the internet to learn how to get one and is confronted with prices far out of her reach, considering up until a week ago she had been dead. She creates a GoFundMe and posts the link on her Instagram page, receiving a dozen donations and hundreds of hateful comments.

On the day of the march, Frida gets an Uber to take her to downtown Detroit. She doesn't know all the details, but she's pieced together the U.S. president in this life is a total pendejo. The park downtown is filled with women wearing pink knit hats shaped into little cat ears, babies holding signs, and white women speaking into bullhorns.

Droves of women hold up posters like works of art that Frida figures took hours to make. Signs say things like "we are the granddaughters of the witches you couldn't burn," "girls just wanna have FUNdamental rights," and "my body, my choice."

Frida smiles at an old woman holding a sign, "I can't believe I still have to protest this shit."

Frida wheels herself alongside the crowd, careful to keep her distance from the others so she won't run over anyone's toes, but the people behind her are pushy, coming as close to her as they can, and trying to worm their way around her. She finds herself dodging gringas in pink hats holding signs that read "feminism is for everybody" and saying sorry to women wearing shirts that say "healthcare is a human right."

Some kind strangers move out of her way or let Frida get in front of them. One woman, wearing a Bernie Sanders sweatshirt, offers to help push her. Frida nods and smiles at the woman, feeling both grateful and like a child. Frida is tempted to ask the woman who Bernie Sanders is but doesn't want to seem even more out of place. Together, Frida and her new caretaker wheel their way along the march route, joining in the chants and cheers of the crowd.

Some women recognize her from Instagram and stand in front of her wheelchair so she can't move past them, asking her for selfies. She half smiles in dozens of photos with women who don't say thank you. When marchers aren't shoving their phones in her face for selfies, Frida overhears them speaking about her.

"She looks so similar to her, you'd think she came back from the dead or something."

"I heard she's a communist."

"She's overhyped. She doesn't even look that much like Frida Kahlo."

Frida tells the woman she no longer needs her help and abandons her wheelchair on the side of the road. Using her stiff limbs, she tries her best to keep up with the more agile marchers but keeps getting bumped. She thinks maybe she should've stayed in the wheelchair after all. Each step on the pavement sends a wave of pain through her body. She is getting exhausted. And hungry.

Frida realizes she hasn't eaten at all since she came back from the dead two weeks ago. She sees a coffee shop on the street, but the thought of drinking a coffee or eating a croissant makes her stomach churn. A woman crashes into Frida, and she smells salty. Better than the tamales she used to serve at dinner parties back when she was still alive. Frida inhales and notices all the marchers smell great.

When the sweat glistening on their necks starts to look appetizing, Frida knows she should leave. She turns to go, and another woman bumps into her, putting her hand on Frida's shoulder, trying to apologize. Frida sinks her teeth into the woman's hand and bites down hard, taking the woman's pointer finger and eating it whole. The woman screams and clutches her hand, blood pouring down her arm.

Frida almost apologizes but can't stop herself from lunging at the woman a second time, taking a bite out of her bicep. The woman runs away screaming. Other women follow suit without knowing what is happening. Frida bites off bits and pieces of the frantic women's bodies, not able to catch anyone in whole, just taking a little bit of them to sustain herself. She bites the neck of a woman wearing a hat with

Frida's face embroidered onto it, jolting the woman so hard it knocks her hat to the ground, where it gets trampled by the fleeing crowd. Screams and cries ring through the air. A woman trips and lands face-first on the pavement, and Frida dives to the ground and takes a bite of her ankle, then her calf, then her thigh. As she goes in for more, she looks up and notices an older woman filming her.

"That's @notfridakahlo!" the woman's daughter says.

Frida leaves the bleeding woman on the ground and pounces at the amateur videographer, knocking the phone out of her hands and biting her fingers off one at a time, delighting in the way the woman yelps each time she takes a bite. The daughter starts running, so Frida pushes the old woman aside and chases her. She screams for help as Frida approaches, and the cops monitoring the event descend onto the crowd, holding their guns to shoot but not daring to risk the lives of the white women in pink pussy hats.

Frida tries her best to blend into the crowd, a sudden human-like instinct to survive kicking in, rivaling only her other, newer instinct to feed. She moves in the opposite direction of the cops, unable to run because of the ache in her body, but still managing to not be seen amongst all the chaos. Any time someone gets close enough to her she takes a small bite. The flesh of dozens of feminists land in her stomach, filling her up.

When she reaches a quieter part of the city, she calls an Uber. She wipes the blood and strands of hair from random women off her face, sits on a bench and waits.

When the driver picks her up, he complains about the "annoying bitches" who "aren't grateful for all the rights men have given them" and how they are "blocking the traffic so they can rally about killing babies." She waits for him to pull into her apartment and say, "is this you?" before pouncing on him. He screams and she goes for his tongue first, because she wants him to shut the hell up. Then she eats his face, spitting out the stubble from his beard. She gorges on his arms, his torso, his legs. His blood and guts decorate the inside of the car, and she leaves him there, ripped open and unmoving for somebody else to find.

She feels a little stronger after eating, strong enough to make it up to her second-floor apartment and run herself a warm bubble bath. Frida slips into the water and looks down at her body. She wiggles her crooked toes, examining her swollen limbs. The skin on her legs is flakier than before, decaying slivers of it floating around her in the water. She isn't sure how much longer she can stay in Detroit, but tonight, she chooses to settle into the warmth surrounding her. The longer she stays in the tub, the pinker the water turns as the blood melts off of her. She scrubs her body clean with a purple bar of soap. She drains the tub, watching the blood and floating skin swim into the pipes.

Polycystic Ovary Syndrome Reimagined

Nothing seemed off until I was fourteen years old, eating handfuls of soil straight from the bag. My mom caught me one day with brown flecks in my braces and called the doctor.

Dr. Moultrie was six feet tall and infinitely more beautiful than I could ever imagine myself being. She began the checkup and I hoped she wouldn't notice the Strawberry Shortcake underwear I was wearing under the paper gown. I didn't want to tell her about all the dirt I'd swallowed. Dr. Moultrie probably never ate anything disgusting in her life.

"When was the last time you had your period?" She asks with certainty, and my face flushes red. When you're fourteen years old, periods are only talked about in whispers. When you're fourteen years old and your period doesn't come for months at a time, you consider it a blessing, but Dr. Moultrie talks about my ailing ovaries and throws around the words "chronic" and "condition" and I zone out thinking about what she would look like with dirt stuck between her perfect teeth.

"Just lower your water intake or the flowers will continue cultivating. They're already filling your uterus," Dr. Moultrie warns me.

It didn't take long for the flowers to grow. One morning I woke with an itch in my throat. I looked in the mirror and opened my mouth wide and there was a trout lily licking my tonsil. I reached a finger to the back of my throat, gagging as I tried to grab the flower. My eyes watered as I yanked it, so I stopped. During science class I coughed up petals. On the bus, I wanted to eat more soil. I could feel my ovaries rolling in my body.

Each week, more flowers accumulated. The throat lilies were now accompanied by some cornflowers and Dutchman's breeches. I tried to laugh less because whenever I did petals would shoot out of my mouth. It had been three months since my last period.

After five months with no period, I woke one morning to a sprout on my chin. Within a few days it blossomed into a whispering dandelion. My brother came up to me while I was staring at it in the bathroom mirror and ripped it off my chin to make a wish; a dot of blood sat where the stem was attached. The next day five more dandelions grew in its place.

After eight months with no period, I visit Dr. Moultrie again. I tried to pluck my chin flowers, but their roots were deeper than ever. She is polite and pretends not to notice the beard, instead asks me if I have any new symptoms, and I open my mouth to reveal the garden in the back of my throat.

Dr. Moultrie pulls long, silver tweezers from her desk drawer and sterilizes them. She sticks the tweezers in my mouth. I want to gag, I want to reject the metal being hoisted where it doesn't belong, but I don't. Dr. Moultrie clasps onto a leg of the Dutchman's breeches and pulls. I feel a pain in my pelvis. It rolls down my back, up my stomach, through my throat, and out comes the flower attached to a three-foot-long stem with a small mass of pink flesh at the roots. I tell her that's enough for the day and go home, cornflowers still populating in my throat.

After Dr. Moultrie pulls the flower out of me, I have a four-week long period. On the last day of my month of bleeding, the moon is full and a clump of my hair falls out. I flush the mass of black hair in the toilet. Two weeks after my month-long period, lupine grows in its place.

Two months after my month-long period, I meet a pink-haired girl at the mall who tells me I smell like her grandmother's house, but she doesn't mind.

"Want to hang out sometime? Can I braid

these?" She gently picks up the flowers flowing from my chin. I write my phone number on her hand using the sparkly red gel pen I have in my tote bag.

Three days after I leave my number on the pink-haired girl's arm, she invites me to her house. We sit under the sequined purple canopy draped over her four-poster bed, and she touches all the flowers growing from my head and my chin. She doesn't think it's gross when the tiny baby's breath fall from my scalp and rests on my shoulders. She turns on Lorde and braids the chin flowers, long enough to touch my belly button.

She asks me to spend the night, and after she falls asleep, I sneak into her parents' garden and eat soil with my bare hands. I haven't eaten soil since before Dr. Moultrie pulled the flower out of me even though I think about it all the time. Soil keeps falling through my fingers, back into the garden, and no matter how much I scoop into my mouth I still want more. I place my face onto the garden bed and eat the soil from the ground.

"What are you doing?"

I look up in the dark to see the pink-haired girl silhouetted by the moon. Soil drops from my bottom lip and gets stuck in the flowers growing from my chin. The pink-haired girl grabs a chunk of soil stuck in my hair and leaves me alone in the garden. Not wanting to face her after she watched me slurp soil, I walk home under the moon's glow, picking the grit from my teeth.

II.
How to Become Enough

Up Next:
I Dye My Hair
Blonde

Curly-haired girls, I promise you this video is going to solve your biggest problems. For those of you who are new here, my name is Xiomara and welcome to my channel *Xo Curl No Mo'*. Some girls have a slew of products meant to uplift, defrizz, add a glossy sheen, and remedy your sadness after your boyfriend dumps you because he can't stand looking at your hair that looks like a home for angry guinea pigs rather than soft strands to run his fingers through. Anyway, I used to spend my days fighting frizz and coaxing my curls to have the perfect spring and bounce, but eventually I realized there was nothing I could do. Then I discovered the CurlNoMore Extra-Strength Flat Iron for Unfortunately Curly Hair™. You can find it at Ulta in the "ethnic hair aisle." The CNMESFIFUCH™ is one of the cheaper straightening products on the market, running at only $799.99—excluding tax. It's worth the investment to tame your hair and ramp up your racial ambiguity. Anyway, let's get started. Before you do anything, you'll want to start with clean hair, which brings me to our curly hair sponsor for this week: CoilFoil™ relaxing shampoo and conditioner. It's filled with curl-flattening chemicals, which gives you a nice head start on straightening it. You'll definitely lose some hair when you initially start using it, but I began using CoilFoil™ about a year ago and it only took my hair six months to adjust. See, right here, where it's still thin in my part? You should've seen the clumps in the drain like small pets swirling away. My mom was mad because I kept clogging the sink and my boyfriend said 'ew,' but now everyone says it's beautiful. You can get it half-off if you follow the link in the description and use my discount code XoCurl50. Anyway, once your hair is clean, put your flat iron on the highest setting. See, it's this one, called CurlBLASTER™. Just press this pink button, and now we wait for heat.

Notice the hot plates are searing orange and billowing with smoke, which is how you know it's ready. Clip your hair into multiple sections to make sure you can access the bottom layers. Start by grabbing a piece of hair, stretching it out until it's as straight as Jake in your political science class who is always complimenting you on how good your English is, and then pinch it between the two hot plates and slide it down to the ends of your hair. Sure, it smells like it's burning, but just ignore that. And the smoke. You might want to take the batteries out of your smoke detector before you do this, because I'm speaking from experience when I say the fire department will not be happy with you when your neighbors call after your smoke detector beeps for two hours straight. I actually just got rid of my smoke alarms altogether since I have to straighten my hair every day. No fires yet. Anyway, keep repeating this over and over to each piece of curly hair you see. Make sure you grab these tricky ones in the back, too. Don't leave any curl untouched. When you get to the pieces closest to your head, your scalp might singe a bit, but that's fine. Also, if you pull a chunk of your hair out in the process, that's fine too. Your hair was probably too thick anyway. Fuck! Sorry, I just clamped my ear in the hot iron. It's fine, it happens a lot. If you look closely at my ears, you'll see a bunch of small white scars, but when my hair is down, which it always is because curly hair looks even worse in a ponytail, you can't see them. Sometimes you'll get a forehead burn too. It's kind of cool to watch your brown skin turn to puffy white. Anyway, just keep fighting your hair. This usually only takes about four hours. If your iron stops smoking, touch your finger to it to make sure it's still hot. If it smells like burning flesh, it's working. Anyway, keep straightening until each strand rolls down your back like silk. Until you can't tell your hair was curly in the first place, forgetting what you looked like with unruly hair. Until your coworkers stop asking what you are, and your boss starts calling you Mara instead of Xiomara because it's easier to pronounce. Keep straightening until the CNMESFIFUCH™ corrals each curl, makes each strand identical to the next. They might fight back a bit but watch how they fall in line anyway.

The Comfort of It

Abuela's house smelled of sazón and strong floral perfume seeping from the rose walls. When I called her from the doorway, she burst into the living room wearing a greasy apron over jeans and a t-shirt I had designed for our family reunion last summer: 'I'm not perfect, but I'm a Casiano, and that's close enough.'

"Oh, my Carmen." She wrapped her soft arms around me, held my face in her hands, and gave me her signature kiss-on-each-cheek-three-times greeting. "Why are you sad?" she asked.

"Ella broke up with me." I tried to shrug it off, but she looked at me like if she made one wrong move I would melt, leaving behind a damp stain on the carpet.

"You should join us tonight," she said, warm arms still holding on. I tried to peel myself from her grasp, shaking my head at her.

After telling my family about my relationship with Ella, I stopped going to family functions. Last Christmas, I went to Abuela's house on the 26th instead. She let me bring Ella along to our makeshift holiday with leftover cookie dough and Christmas movies. I hadn't been to my childhood home since I moved out a few months ago into an off-campus apartment. I didn't visit my family during school breaks; I stayed in my apartment and stared at blank walls—blank walls because I didn't want to put up photos of people who didn't want me, blank walls because full ones would remind me of the holiday celebrations and family vacations I was no longer a part of.

I knew La Noche de San Juan shouldn't be different. I didn't want to risk it turning a night of washing away your bad omens into a night of creating new ones. I'd always loved the holiday—gathering with my family at Sturgeon Lake to wash away different problems each year—Cousin Izzy's bad grades, Tío Mike's back pain, or even, one time, Tía Ana's affair.

When I was younger, I never had anything in mind. I would submerge myself into the water just to feel the comfort of it. As I got older, I started using La Noche to rid myself of animosity from failed friendships, rejection from my first-choice college, and fights with my mom over whether I should move out right away. Last year, I tried freeing myself of my feelings for Ella, but instead I asked her out the next day. I looked at my grandmother's pleading face, and I remembered how good the holiday always made me feel.

"They're getting better," Abuela looked down at her feet, "I promise."

"You're sure?" I asked and Abuela nodded and led me to the kitchen for lunch where she knew—full of warm carbs—I would comply.

I drove Abuela and myself to the lake at dusk. She brought coolers full of beer and sliced fruit, and I was tasked with rolling them down to the lakeside. The familiar smell of burning wood and the sounds of laughter and Spanglish led me towards a small campfire, surrounded by close to thirty family members.

Last Thanksgiving, in the middle of prayer, Mami announced to the family they all needed to pray for my eternal soul, and they did, right around the turkey and cranberry sauce I spent hours helping them prepare. Abuela was the only one who followed me when I left the dining room, forcing myself not to wonder if they were right.

The next eight months my family blocked me out, leaving more room for Ella to come in. My apartment walls transformed into a gallery of Ella and me: sprawled out on an afghan on the campus lawn, eating candied apples at the carnival in town, wearing ball gowns at her sorority formal, and walking the beach in Santa Monica during spring break. If Ella and I weren't together, I would either visit Abuela—always during odd times of the day to ensure I wouldn't accidentally show up when someone else was visiting— or I would be alone in my apartment, teaching myself how to crochet. I crocheted a five-foot scarf when Ella went home for two weeks while Abuela was visiting family in Puerto Rico.

I took a deep breath and rolled the coolers to the commotion at the shore. I placed them down with a thud and everyone's heads shot up. Cousins leaned over to aunts and uncles and second cousins and whispered and shook their heads and one uncle grabbed his daughter's hand and pulled—pulled her towards the lake, pulled her as close as they could get without breaking the sacred boundary of the water's edge. The wind whistled through the trees, picked up my family's whispers—*she's too pretty to be gay* and *she just hasn't met the right man yet and it's because her mami sent her to a bullshit liberal arts college*— and whisked them away, deep into the forest and lake. Mami scrunched her face at me.

"Carmen, I haven't heard from you in a while," she said, staring at the blue cooler.

"Here's the food," I gestured to the two coolers I had been pulling behind my back, as if she hadn't already seen them. Everyone swarmed over, picking through the contents, and paying no attention to me. My uncle, Raymond, walked along the crowd, holding hands with a blond woman.

"Meet my girlfriend, Hannah," he said to Mami. I watched my mom's icy stance I had gotten used to over the past eight months melt into an approachable shrug as she reached her arms out to embrace this new woman, providing me the opportunity to sneak off to the lake.

The sun was setting in melting sorbet hues and the lake was calm. Ripping grass from the dirt, I thought about what my relationship with Ella had cost me. I used to go to the flea market with Mami, watching her haggle the vendors for an even greater discount on already discounted wall art and lamps and then, depending on how much money she was able to save, we would decide if we were going to get lunch from our favorite taco truck or go all out and go to Olive Garden. She made my first Communion dress, sewing in dozens of small daisy shaped beads I'd spent thirty minutes selecting from A.C. Moore. My mom, who once loved me more than anyone, now thought I was disgraceful because I fell in love with Ella, who left me anyway.

Falling in love with her seemed worth it. I asked her to be my girlfriend at this same lake. The October air pricked our noses. Sitting on a blue blanket my mother made, we ate peanut butter sandwiches and drank hot chocolate from insulated cups as golden leaves floated in the wind.

It was perfect until Ella tried posting a picture of us on Instagram, getting quiet when I called her in the middle of the night and begged her to take it down so my family wouldn't see. Ella told me she came out to her parents when she was sixteen and they were fine with it, which made me feel brave, so I told my family on Thanksgiving morning during a commercial break of the *Macy's Thanksgiving Day*

I looked up from the lake when I heard the shuffling of grass and saw my cousin Benny's black Air Jordans, perfect and creaseless with purple laces. He plopped down next to me and pulled out a cigarette.

"So, you've been ostracized from La Noche too, huh cuz?" he said before taking a drag. Benny had just been released from nine months in prison for selling weed last year. We were the prime duo of disappointments to our Catholic family: the stoner and the lesbian. He handed me a beer from his backpack. I cracked it open and drank as José Feliciano songs played and harmonized with the laughter of my family.

"'Buela told me you're here because Ella dumped you."

"She's not the relationship type."

"After midnight we start fresh." He took another drag and patted my knee.

"I shouldn't have even come tonight." I picked at the label on my bottle.

"I'm glad you came because if you hadn't, everybody would've been hating on the convict instead," he said. I hit his arm lightly and he clutched it, pretending it hurt.

The ritual began at midnight. At 11:30 Benny and I joined our family at the shore. I slipped off my pink dress to reveal my bathing suit—a tankini and shorts. I kept it modest. I'll be damned if my family called me a dyke and a slut.

As time passed, family members inched closer to the shore. Benny and I stayed off to the side for as long as possible, talking about his new job at Lowe's. How he hated mixing paint and helping customers compare shades of white, but it was one of the only jobs he could get with a record. I told him about my new apartment. Mami ended up near us and I saw her staring at Benny and I talking.

She leaned over to Raymond and said, "Some of us have a lot to wash away tonight." She looked over at us, the family fuckups.

I stared at the ground, trying to act like I didn't know she was talking about me. I tried not to think about the masses I went to as a kid, or what my family said to me around the Thanksgiving turkey. I tried not to let them be right. Benny squeezed my hand.

"Don't worry about what they think," he said.

"Right. You'll just have God to answer to," Mami piped up.

Benny squeezed my hand tighter, but I pulled it away from him, turned towards my mom, and forced her to look at her daughter for the first time in months.

"I don't care what God thinks."

"You should start."

"Why can't you treat me like you used to?" She looked down at her bare feet. In the silence sat Mami's declaration I was going to Hell. In the silence sat the following weeks of me praying for hours each night in the hopes I could change until dark circles bruised my face.

"I just want the best for you." I dodged her hand as it reached for my shoulder.

Cousins and aunts and uncles looked at their start cleansing. Abuela was finally the one who stepped between the two of us, putting an arm around my shoulder.

"It's time," she said, waving her hands in the air to make sure everyone saw her. "Let's count."

The collective voice of my family floated to the treetops as we counted *diez, nueve, ocho, siete, seis, cinco, cuatro*, placing so much emphasis on the ritual meant to make our problems go away. You could almost hear the aching hope I would become something they could understand as we shouted *tres, dos, uno… ¡dale!*

Everyone leaned backwards into the lake, trusting the cool embrace of the water would catch them. The water surrounded me, chilling my blue painted toenails. The silence beneath the surface gave me the space I needed to think, to wish. I felt my body pulling towards the surface, pulling towards air. I came up a moment too soon. The midnight sky was blurry, obscured by the water stuck to my lashes.

There wasn't much time to breathe before we went back down. The icy water sloshed around as our bodies submerged. Underwater I saw my cousins, aunts, uncles, thirty bodies sinking down, legs flailing as they tried to find a space in the lake to claim as their own. Thirty bodies touched the lake floor. Thirty bodies hoped the cold water and the rough-pebbled ground would help them become themselves. Dread washed over me. I ached for air. Maybe I should be ashamed. I ached to get out of the water.

I threw my body backwards one last time and went under. I imagined the waves draining the pain from my pores, taking it out to the lake. I sunk deeper into the water until I hit the bottom. The water moved around me, but I was still, my body finding its place. I came up last and watched as some relatives choked a bit from inhaling water during their abrupt departure. Water rushed off my body as I clambered to the shore. Everyone began hugging each other and laughing, talking about how new they felt.

I stood off to the side, without a towel and shivering. By the shore I saw the outline of Benny and his dad hugging. Just as I was turning to head back to the car and wait for Abuela to finish saying her goodbyes to everyone, Mami came to me. In silence, she peeled the damp towel from her palm-tree-swimsuit-covered torso and draped it over my shoulders. I shook it off and let it fall into the dirt with a wet thump.

Becoming Beyoncé in Three Easy Steps!

The first thing you're going to want to do is get off the couch. I have a friend who has a friend who has a cousin who catered for one of Beyoncé's parties, and they told me Beyoncé never sits. Sitting slows you down.

There you go, you're up now. Smooth out your holey Walmart t-shirt with bleach stains on the shoulder, and let's get to work.

The truth is, anybody can be Beyoncé, but nobody is willing to put in the effort. People are lazy. We all have the same twenty-four hours in a day—we just have to learn how to manipulate each minute.

Sure, there's Jules and Spencer to care for, but

Beyoncé has three kids. Sure, you have a house to take care of because your husband doesn't know how to work a vacuum cleaner, but Beyoncé has an entire mansion. Are you done making excuses yet? If you are, come with me on this journey of 3 steps you can take to be just like Beyoncé.

Step #1: Make yourself have scheduling conflicts so you seem more wanted.

Beyoncé is impossible to reach because she's always jetting around town using her time wisely and getting shit done. She charges enough money per performance to send every kid in your town to college and then some, and she accomplished this through making herself scarce. You don't have a busy enough schedule to be as hard to reach as Beyoncé yet, because you are just learning what dedication and time management are, but you can always pretend until it becomes real. Schedule two things at once: you have to take Spencer to his ballet class across town at the same time you have to take Jules to her swim meet. Tell them not only did you double book them but, there's a third and more important event you have to attend, leaving both calling all of their friends' parents in the desperate hope for a ride. Make your presence in your children's life scarce and soon you'll be turning everyone down.

Step #2: Find something to believe in.

Beyoncé's lucky number is four and it has followed

her throughout her entire career. Some might say if her lucky number was 5 or 72 she would've fallen to obscurity, just like the other members of Destiny's Child, but since she chose something to believe in, she was able to become Beyoncé. And you can too.

It doesn't have to be a divine number. It could be anything you can make into your entire personality and "accidentally" stumble upon in your daily life to use as a sign. Purple, like the color of Jules' favorite stuffed animal. Daisies, which you buy yourself once a week since your husband won't. Or how about a monarch that butterfly, which your father always said was a sign your dead mother was nearby? The trick is to make sure it's something you run into often and post online every time you see it so people think you have some kind of power or luck. If they think you do, they will start treating you so.

Step #3: Be a critic and a player.

Every night before she goes to bed, Beyoncé grabs a glass of wine and winds down by watching video clips of her performances for several hours with an intern nearby, taking notes.

Get your kids in this habit too. Record Spencer's dance lessons and performances. Point out the roll of fat sticking out underneath the armpit of his leotard. Point out the way he stumbles a bit on his plie. Tell him there's only twelve years until dance school application season and if he doesn't get into Juilliard then what's the point of all of this?

Record yourself at work. Watch how often you

ignore new emails. Watch yourself wonder whether the pivot table you've worked on for four hours even matters. When you finally get around to answering your emails—after gossiping with your coworker Mary, who you don't like, for forty-five minutes—count how many exclamation marks you put in each message. Seven in one paragraph? Are you kidding? Next, watch how you make love to your husband. You seem so tired, not even taking off his shirt before going down on him. You're wearing underwear you've owned for ten years. You should put on more of a show. Play back when you burnt chicken for the kids. Jules didn't eat at all that night. They deserve better meals. They deserve a better mother. Realize you could be doing so much better. Yes. Keep going. This is good. Realize you aren't enough. Figure out how to become enough.

You Could Be That Kind of Girl

Isa's mother, Lydia, always told Isa the secret to staying skinny was to trick your body. She told her this the first time when Isa gained ten pounds after hitting puberty in the seventh grade. Lydia showed her how to take fifteen grapes and cut them in half before eating them with a fork.

"So now it's like I have thirty grapes?" Isa asked, as she tried to understand her mom's logic on an empty stomach.

"Twice the grapes with half the calories," her mom popped a grape half into her mouth and left the rest for Isa to eat while she imagined her body half its size.

Now, Isa straightens her carefully curated first-day-of-vacation sundress—a yellow babydoll dress with pink flowers splattered across it and thin straps that show her freckled shoulders—before she sits down next to her mom and her cousin, Sammi.

Isa looks at the food in front of her—eggs, a slice of toast, and a little bowl of fruit. She cuts the fruit into pieces and puts a small square of cantaloupe on her tongue. The juice seeps into her taste buds.

She watches as Sammi, thirteen and angular, shoves eggs into her mouth, a piece of melted cheese hanging from her bottom lip. Her curly hair puffs around her head and she is wearing canvas shorts so long they touch the tops of her knees. Isa can't help but think about how Sammi is wasting her skinniest years wearing boy's clothes. But as the thought slithers into Isa's mind, it is drowned out with waves of self-appointed anger for projecting her problems onto her cousin.

*

Lydia examines her daughter and niece from across the island as they eat breakfast. She loves them and considers both hers as Sammi's mom—Lydia's sister Sophia—is, in Lydia's eyes, hardly an appropriate example of womanhood for Sammi. Lydia witholds disdain for Sammi's bad outfit and frizzy hair. She hopes Sammi will grow into her looks the way she did when she was Sammi's age; the way Isa did when she was that age, too.

Lydia looks at Isa, happy to be with her daughter for the first time in months since Isa got a photography job in the city. She looks at her face, the face she has loved since birth. The face she has loved since birth had a giant smudge of mascara on its nose. She thinks of all the catching up she wants to do with Isa, all the questions she wants to ask her. The list shimmies in her head—Isa, how's your job going? Isa, do you miss living near the beach? Isa, how's it going with the girl you've been dating?—not to mention how much she loves Isa's dress.

"You have a giant smudge of mascara on your nose," stumbles out of Lydia's mouth instead. Isa runs to the bathroom before Lydia has an opportunity to say any of the things she wants to say to her.

Sophia comes by then, dirty hair sitting in a nest on top of her head, her soft body hidden under worn out gray sweatpants and a holey t-shirt with the Clemson University logo on it, to get more toast for Sammi's brother, Ernesto.

"Sammi sweetie, did you get enough to eat?" Sophia asks.

"Don't worry Soph, I took care of my girls," Lydia says and pats Sammi on the back. Sophia scoops more eggs on Sammi's plate and kisses her cheek. Lydia doesn't think Sophia should be encouraging her daughter to eat so much. Especially at this age, when girls like her can get big so quickly.

Isa rejoins Lydia and Sammi. Lydia notices Isa glancing at Sammi's refilled plate. Sammi continues to eat her eggs for a moment, but then slows down and glances at Isa and Lydia's twin plates, still seemingly as full as before. Sammi places her fork down and looks up at Isa and Lydia, butter smeared on her left cheek.

"Will y'all come swimming with me later? I'm sick of swimming with Ernesto, he always snaps my strap," Sammi asks.

"Yeah, sure," Isa says. "And tell Ernesto to fuck off."

"Isa!" Lydia smacks her arm. Sammi's face swells with held-in laughter.

"Tía, will you come with us?"

"I ate a bit too much breakfast to put on a bikini," she says and rubs her flat stomach like pregnant women do. "But you girls have a great time."

Lydia takes Isa's plate as she gets up from the table and clears the rest of their eggs and toast into the trash.

*

"Can I wear your goggles? I want to see if there's any fish down there."

Sammi puts her hand out to Isa before she is given an answer. Sammi has never doubted Isa's willingness to give parts of herself to her. Isa drops the cool plastic into Sammi's hand.

Sammi ties her frizzy hair into a bun, adjusts her black one-piece suit, and plunges into the water. She ignores the salt water seeping into her goggles and pricking her eyes. She wades through seaweed as she feels the sand on the ocean floor with her fingertips. She sees Isa's long brown legs—muscular and strong—motor past the lazy fish bobbing around in the water.

Sammi had spent hours reading books about the types of wildlife found at South Carolina beaches leading up to the trip, so she recognizes the fish Isa is outswimming as triplefins. She imagines herself as a triplefin, tiny and oval, never catching up to the beautiful girl swimming past.

"I was kinda hoping I'd see a jellyfish." Sammi says after they come up for air.

"They don't come this close to land," Isa says. Sammi thinks back to her research; pictures of gray-pink jellyfish suctioned to the bodies of beachgoers.

*

On the second day of vacation, Sophia makes breakfast. While she cooks, Ernesto runs around the house screaming at full volume, giving Lydia a headache. When Isa and Sammi find their way to the kitchen, Lydia pulls them into an empty hallway.

"I think it's time we ditch," Lydia says.

"Shopping?" Isa asks.

Lydia imagines buying Sammi appropriate clothes for a girl her age, not the too-big worn out t-shirt she is wearing.

"We'll leave after breakfast," Lydia says. Isa and Sammi nod.

Sophia hands each of them a plate overflowing with scrambled eggs loaded with cheese oozing off the side, four slices of toast glistening with butter, and three pieces of bacon. Lydia does the math in her head and guesses the meal is at least 740 calories. They sit down at the sticky island to eat their food. Lydia takes a slice of toast and breaks it into smaller pieces. She watches as Sammi eats half a slice of bacon in one bite. Isa stabs at the eggs and puts a small piece into her mouth.

*

Isa is on her third bite of eggs, thinking about when she should stop, thinking about how she doesn't want to be bloated for the shopping trip, when she looks over and sees Sammi tearing her toast to shreds, chewing slowly. Isa guesses the meal is at least 720 calories. Isa wonders if Sammi knows each bite of toast is about ten calories and that breaking her food into small pieces could make her skinny.

She doesn't want Sammi to spend her life wondering which bite should be her last, so Isa picks up a piece of bacon and takes a big bite. Isa knows she will have to go on an extra-long run tomorrow to make up for the indulgence. Isa feels Lydia nudge her under the table, signaling to Isa she isn't acting ladylike enough. Isa ignores her mother, swallows another piece of bacon, and tries not to cry.

*

Sammi notices how Lydia and Isa eat— small bites, lots of control, no crumbs piling up in their laps. Pretty women behave this way, and Sammi wants to be pretty like Isa and Lydia. But then, Isa starts eating in bigger bites and Sammi copies her still, not understanding the method but wanting to do whatever Isa does. Sammi puts aside her tiny toast bite and picks up a whole slice of toast, taking a big chunk off the corner.

When they get to the mall, Sammi walks to the extra-small rack and watches Isa walk to the medium rack, and she feels a bit of pride swell up in her. She feels out of place in this store, filled with trendy clothes. Sammi's cargo shorts look bulky and drab next to the breezy fabrics and floral patterns. She breezes through the dresses in her size, hating the idea of her in them. Instead, she goes to the medium rack and helps Isa look, quickly finding a yellow dress with white flowers embroidered onto the straps.

"You've gotta try this on," Sammi shoves it toward Isa, knowing her cousin will look perfect in it. Disregarding her cousin's hesitation, Sammi pulls Isa towards the dressing room. Lydia follows them, a pair of blue jeans in hand.

Lydia and Isa emerge from the dressing room at the same time standing in front of a mirror showing every side of themselves. Simultaneously, they turn to the side and look at themselves in the mirror, holding their breath, laying a hand flat on their stomachs. Sammi stands straighter as she looks at her cousin and aunt, thinking about how beautiful they are, wondering if she will ever be beautiful, too. A sigh escapes Isa like air coming out of a deflated balloon.

"I look like a whale. No, a lemon. One of those lemons grown by farmers who are trying to break records for the size of their fruit. I'm the world's largest lemon." Isa crosses her arms over her stomach.

"That's not even the color of a lemon," Lydia says.

*

When they return from the mall, Isa challenges Sammi to a race. Sammi doesn't hesitate to accept the challenge, even though she's pretty sure Isa is faster than her.

"I'm so ready to win," Isa says. She tightens her bikini straps until they cut into her shoulders.

"Tía, will you watch us and see who wins?"

"Alright. Y'all are going to the buoys and back." She counts down from three and the race begins, Isa immediately finding the lead.

Sammi swallows water as she flails around trying to catch up to Isa, always trying to catch up to Isa. She tries to steady her stroke and come up for air but gets too anxious when she sees Isa's legs underwater, once again outswimming triplefins. Sammi pumps her legs, thighs burning, and begs her body to move faster. It isn't long before Sammi passes Isa, and she believes she is finally getting where she needs to be.

*

As Isa swims, the heavy breakfast pulls at her gut. The water ripples around her as Sammi catches up. The dress Sammi picked out for her looked awful. She keeps adjusting her slipping bikini strap. Flames rip through her bicep but she tries to push through her tired, screaming muscles.

Isa feels herself slowing down, and realizes she is swimming with just one arm. Pain burns through her veins. She slams her feet into the ocean floor. Sand wedges up beneath her toenails, and she emerges from the water, sputtering and gasping for air. She looks down to see a bulbous, gelatinous being suction cupped to her upper arm.

*

Lydia is the first to notice Isa struggling in the

water, the first to see her come up for air with a jellyfish on her arm. She runs to her daughter.

Lydia leads Isa to the shore and Sammi trails close behind. Ernesto and Sophia notice the commotion and meet them at the edge of the beach, unhelpful onlookers. Lydia stares at the stinger on her daughter's arm and imagines it sucking out everything from inside of her until she is a sack of bones.

When they make it to land, Lydia pushes Isa to the floor and rips at the stinger.

"You're supposed to pee on it!" Ernesto says.

"Ernesto, get me my water bottle," Lydia points in the direction of her bag.

"Saltwater works better." Sammi looks at the wound instead of Lydia.

Lydia has lived near the beach her entire life. Like most problems, she knows how to fix this.

Ernesto presses the water bottle into Lydia's hand. She flips the cap off and dumps ice-cold water onto the sting. Isa pushes the water bottle away and clasps her arm.

Sammi runs to the ocean and fills up a bucket with saltwater. She dumps it onto Isa's arm.

"Sammi, you're going to hurt her." Lydia grabs the bucket. She's never seen her niece act so defiant. But then Lydia looks at Isa, who is no longer squeezing her arm.

When they get back up to the house, the Rodriguez-Castellanos' surround Isa, asking what is wrong, asking if she is going to die, telling her she should pee on her wound, and asking Lydia what she's going to do about it.

"Sammi is the one who is taking care of Isa," Lydia says, a little embarrassed to admit her ignorance to the family. The family turns to Sammi and starts asking her questions, which she answers as she dabs a washcloth soaked in vinegar on her cousin's arm. They all watch Sammi work on the wound, and it already seems like the swelling is going down.

Fiona Apple Joins Our Crochet Club

Fiona Apple comes to the first meeting of the new year in gray sweatpants, a men's winter coat, brown beanie, and sunglasses covering half of her face, tracking in a trail of murky snow. It's our fault for hanging a flier on the bulletin board of Shriekin' Beans Coffee Shop, where we hold our meetings. She sits in a chair next to Jeanne, the oldest member whose, specialty is vagina art. Fiona rifles through her worn-out green tote bag and pulls out a tangled ball of brown yarn followed by some sort of half-finished stuffed animal. Instead of speaking to us, she begins to work on her tangles with fast fingers.

"Looks like we have a new member of the pack," Jeanne says, bright white dentures beaming at us. She pulls out her current project—a granny square blanket made up entirely of crochet vaginas. "What's your name, sweetie?" She puts a hand on Fiona's shoulder. Fiona scoots her chair several inches away, leaving Jeanne's hand dangling in the air.

"That's not as subversive as you think it is," Fiona says, waving her crochet hook towards her blanket. Jeanne laughs, clutches the blanket closer to her chest.

The rest of us continue to chatter about the upcoming snowstorm, PTA meetings, and town events, while Fiona sits in silence, tapping her foot on the hardwood floor. By the end of the hour, Fiona has completed a two-headed dog. The dog on the left is a light brown pit bull, and the dog on the right is a black pit bull. Its body is a marbled pattern of the two colors, swirling together in a mixture so intricate, it would have taken any of us weeks to finish. The dog has a purple collar around its neck. Jeanne smiles warmly at Fiona as she watches her weave in the ends of her two-headed monstrosity.

"What did you make there, sweetie?" she asks.

"Janet and Mercy. Janet's dead. I have her bones on my mantle at home." She says all of this without looking up at Jeanne, tapping her hook rhythmically on her temple.

The next week Fiona comes in with her crocheted two-headed dog on a real leash, pulling it behind her. She sits it down by her feet and puts bowls of food and water bowl in front of it.

"Can I pet them?" Jeanne asks, her hand hovering slightly over her thigh, hesitant. We aren't sure why she is offering.

Fiona smiles and pushes the dog towards her. Jeanne pats its head lightly. Fiona wriggles it under Jeanne's hand. She makes little panting noises like a happy dog.

Encouraged by this, instead of weirded out like the rest of us, Jeanne pets harder, calling the dog a good girl and scratching its ears. She moves her hand under one of the dog's chins and Fiona begins barking and lunging the stuffed dog at Jeanne's hand. Its plush heads flail from left to right as a guttural growl comes from Fiona. Jeanne pulls her hand away in disbelief. We are silent for the next hour. Every few minutes, Fiona talks to her dog or pets it. She's crocheting a sweater for it.

The next week, Fiona doesn't show up right away. We take this as our opportunity to say what we have all been thinking: Fiona Apple is a freak.

"We should've known as soon as she told us she kept her dog's bones in her house."

"Or what about the giant coat she always wears? It's cold, but you don't see us walking around in menswear."

"Has anyone noticed she always smells kind of funky?"

"I heard she hasn't left her house since 2012."

"She's a bitch." says Jeanne. We are all surprised to hear her join in the chain of hate towards Fiona. "I don't want her in the club anymore," Jeanne continues as we feel a gust of prickly winter air and hear the rustling of a coat and look up to see Fiona has entered Shriekin' Beans, her crocheted pet trailing behind her, its face covered in mud and chunks of salt from the sidewalk. Everyone stops talking and our silence is louder than our gossip.

She keeps her coat on as she sits down, brushes some dirt off her dog's face and pulls out the sweater she had been working on last week.

"Fiona! We were worried you weren't going to come, how are you?" Jeanne says, clearly overcompensating.

"Just lovely, Jeanne. Thanks!" We glance at one another, brace ourselves for an outburst. We expect a tantrum of sorts, an attack from her two-headed dog, but instead she is being the politest she has been since she started crocheting with us.

"How's she doing?" Megan gestures at the dog. Fiona hasn't pulled out the bowl for them this time. When Megan draws attention to it, Fiona uses her heel to slide it under her chair.

"It's just a stuffed animal," her lips turn up in a quiet smirk. She doesn't seem proud of her creation like she did last week. She crumples up the sweater she is working on and pulls out a fresh ball of powder pink yarn. She begins crocheting a beanie. A human sized beanie. She finishes it by the end of the hour and gives it to Jeanne with no comment.

Jeanne holds the hat lightly between her fingertips. Fiona nods but keeps looking at Jeanne. She realizes what Fiona wants from her and pulls the hat over her hair, and the ends curl out of the bottom. Fiona's lips curl into an almost smile.

After she leaves, we all sort of feel bad for how we treated Fiona. The next week when she comes to class, we each have our own crocheted pet by our feet on leashes. Megan has a tabby cat with a cast on its left leg, Jeanne has a colorful parrot, Amy has a raccoon, and the others have various common dogs and cats, modeled after the pets they own. When Fiona stumbles in ten minutes late, her two-headed dog is not following behind her, and she is wearing a thin black coat in serious need of a lint brush. She looks at our new pets, one at a time, eyes lingering. She stops at Jeanne's, perched on her shoulder. She blinks twice. Shifts from heel to heel.

"What's this?" She asks.

"We were all texting the other day when we decided we wanted our own crochet buddies, too." Jeanne pats her parrot on the head and whispers something into its ear. Fiona stares at us, tapping her fingers against her thigh one at a time. We watch her, eager to see how she'll respond to our kind gesture.

Fiona's body stills. She drops her tote bag to the ground. Her face looks pink and blotchy as she turns away from us, walking out of the coffee shop, a gust of wind hitting our faces as she exits. Jeanne picks up the bag and pulls out handfuls of crocheted hats, one for each of us.

Loose Blood

My mortal boyfriend, Kyle, always smells like garlic. So tonight at dinner when I ask my mom if he can come over to watch the season finale of The Bachelor with me, she gives me the face universal to all mothers letting me know if I want this, I will have to fight for it.

"He got a new cologne to cover the smell because he knows it bothers you," I say.

"Why can't you just find a nice vampire boy to date?" My dad says, his dark hair damp from his post-work shower, pearl white hands still stained black from motor oil as he slurps blood from a soup spoon.

"Or at least a mortal boy who doesn't work at such an awful place," Mom says between sips of blood, which she prefers to drink out of a straw.

Kyle works at The Garlic, an awful kitschy

Italian restaurant down by the beach. They literally use cloves of garlic as decorations. Bushels of it hang from the ceiling. It's gross.

"Yeah, Ava, how do you stand it?" My sister Izzy says in between sips of blood from a soup bowl. She drinks more blood than my mom and I combined and is almost as tall as our dad even though she is just twelve.

"Because I love him, you idiot," I say back. Of course I can smell Kyle. His scent burns my nose. When we make out in his room my clothes reek for weeks, after dozens of washes. But I don't care. It's a good burn.

My parents don't understand how I can spend so much time with a mortal and not kill him. Killing humans to feed is illegal, but the humans legalized the consumption of loose blood, which my dad buys from Barry's Blood Bank, a shop where poor humans sell small portions of their blood for a couple of bucks.

"The Mortons have a son your age," Mom says. I roll my eyes at her. Timmy Morton is skinny and pale and works with his parents at their funeral home. He's a total stereotype.

"Just because I'm a vampire doesn't mean I need to date another vampire."

"I know, honey. I just think it would be easier for you."

"And us." Dad snorts.

People at school used to give me weird looks and cross the hallway when they passed me, sometimes holding up crosses or garlic cloves as they passed. Until I started dating Kyle. He isn't the coolest guy in school, but he is on the varsity soccer team which gives me some credit among the cool kids.

"You guys just don't get it." My parents grew up in a neighborhood full of vampires and could date anyone they wanted. My only option for a vampire boyfriend is Timmy. And I won't settle. I finish my blood in silence and go back up to my bedroom to text Kyle.

Come over. Through the window. Extra cologne.

Twenty minutes later I hear rustling in the bushes. I throw down the rope ladder I keep under my bed to sneak him in. He's clumsy on the ladder, but I hold it steady for him.

I turn on The Bachelor and watch Kyle watch it. He seems bored at first, but once I start explaining to him the plot and betrayal of all the contestants, he begins to lean towards the TV, shaking his head in disapproval when a long-legged brunette calls a long-legged blonde a gold digger. I've been obsessed with *The Bachelor* the past few months because I think it's fun to watch rich mortals waste their wealth and mortality. Imagine having everything going for you, but having to go on a shiny, plastic television show to find love. I'm lucky. My love is in my bed.

The show ends, so naturally, we decide to make out for a while. His mouth is working its way down my neck when I catch the sound of my parents arguing. I shush Kyle, though he's not making noise. He moves his mouth away from my neck and sits next to me in silence, trying to hear what my parents are saying, their voices growing. I send Kyle home and go downstairs to see what's going on, but when I reach the bottom of the stairs, they are no longer yelling, instead they are putting on their coats.

"We have some errands to run," Mom says. My parents rarely leave the house after dark. Humans don't take well to vampires roaming around at night, and my family's bright red eyes and translucent skin don't do us any favors when trying to blend in.

"Can I come?" Izzy asks, walking down the stairs, still a little too young to understand people hate us.

"Kiddo, you have so much homework to finish," Dad responds and ruffles her hair, leaving the bright black strands pointing upwards in various directions.

"Ava, you reek," Izzy says. I glare at her, but our parents don't seem to notice.

They leave the house after nightfall, and we don't see them until breakfast. Their eyes are bruised with lack of sleep, and scratches cover my dad's face. My mom has matching ones on her arms. They set bowls of blood out for us, but it is dark purple and smells rancid.

"What the hell is this?" Izzy sniffs her bowl.

"Animal blood," Dad says, grimacing as he takes the first sip. "Barry has raised his prices and I haven't been getting as much work at the shop, so this is what we've got."

I drink my blood, holding back disgust as the slimy, dark matter drips down my throat. This is okay for now. This will have to be okay.

"You need to help me find a job," I say to Kyle at school later.

"The Garlic is hiring, actually. A bunch of people quit and they're, like, desperate for replacements," Kyle says. "I'll tell my boss about you."

Two hours later, I get a call from a number I don't recognize.

"Can you start tonight, kid?" says a gruff voice from the other end.

"Huh?"

"Ken said you were looking for a job?"

"You mean Kyle?"

"Come in at 6." The phone cut off.

I walk into The Garlic wearing a pair of black jeans and a thin black turtleneck. At the entrance, a host hesitantly greets me.

"I'm a new employee," I say.

"Oh, hey! Let's take you back to see Bill. I'm Vanessa, by the way."

"Ava," I respond. I follow Vanessa back through the restaurant and into the kitchen. There are only a few employees, and they all look like they're in the greatest rush of their lives. The garlic scent gets worse the further into the kitchen we go, and tears begin streaming down my face. I try wiping them with my sleeve when Vanessa isn't looking.

"Bill! She's here," Vanessa shouts towards a slightly open office door and leaves me standing in the middle of the kitchen. As workers whip past me, I feel obtrusive. A few minutes later, a man sticks his bald head out of the office door.

"Are ya coming in or what?" I recognize the voice from the phone. I walk into his office and sit down on a tiny folding chair in the corner. The office is the size of a broom closet and hardly fits a desk with a rolling chair that Bill, a large man, is shoved into in a way I imagine is uncomfortable.

"Alright, so we need someone to be a server, or a hostess. Or maybe both. You think you could—" he looks up at me for the first time, familiar glint of recognition in his eyes as he realizes what I am. "But what we really need is a dishwasher. You know how to wash dishes, kid?"

I've never washed a dish in my life. In my house we have one dish for each of us and just throw them in the dishwasher each day. But I can't lose this job before I've even started. I nod. He leads me to the back of the kitchen.

"It's pretty self-explanatory. You scrape the food into the trash, place the dishes in the rack, and when it's full you run the dishwasher through. Easy peasy. Anyone could do it."

I sit by the sink for the next five hours, getting food and water all over my turtleneck because I'm too afraid to ask Bill for an apron. I scrape clumps of cold tomato sauce and half eaten noodles into the trash. Everything burns.

At the end of my shift my hands are dry and red, and my clothes are a mess. My hair curls around my face, sweaty and sudsy. I worked for 5 hours tonight. I do the math in my head as I walk home. 36.25 before taxes. Barely enough to buy loose blood for one day.

When I get home after 1AM, I'm surprised to find my parents waiting for me.

"Where the—" my mom starts to ask but then she gags. "Ava, you smell awful. Were you with Kyle?"

"I got a job at The Garlic. Why are you guys awake?"

"We want you focused on"—Dad gags—"school. Not some job." Dad gags and motions for me to go upstairs, away from his raw, red nose.

The servers buzz around before the dinner rush. I try to find Bill to ask him for an apron, but he isn't in his office, so I work without one. Halfway through my shift I remember I have a history test in first period the next morning. A test I've barely studied for. I stand over the sink, trying to remember the dates and terms I'm meant to know for tomorrow, trying to wash the dishes, trying to keep my sweater clean.

When I get home my mom is dressing a large gash on my dad's arm. A pitcher of fresh animal blood sits on the kitchen table. They don't comment on how I smell. We don't say goodnight. I stay up the rest of the night and go over my notes for the test tomorrow, watching the sun rise as I force my eyes to stay open.

Not long after the rest of my family wakes up and begins getting ready for the day, Kyle knocks on our front door.

"I heard you got off work late again. Last minute study session?" he asks.

We sit on the couch, quizzing each other on vocabulary terms while my family drinks animal blood in the other room. When Izzy finishes her blood, she comes into the living room and turns on the TV. As we study and the TV blares, Izzy is looking down at her hands, picking her fingers and tossing small scraps of skin to the ground.

"You okay?" I ask, and Izzy snaps. She leaps up from the couch, her now glazed-over eyes twitching. She locks eyes with Kyle and makes her away across the room in one bound, lunging on top of him. Kyle squirms under Izzy's weight, and I watch horrified at my normally gentle sister's actions. It takes me too long to react. I try pulling her off Kyle, but she's stronger than me. Izzy, who is growing into herself, who is unaware of the power she has, unaware of how aggressive she can be because our parents always raised us to be soft despite our strength, continues clawing at my boyfriend.

"Dad!" I yelp towards the kitchen, and he arrives, barely capable of pulling Izzy off Kyle. Izzy is vibrating, a low growl escaping her chest. Our dad restrains her, drags her far across the room from Kyle. Her face drops.

"Kyle I'm—"

He grabs his things and trips over himself trying to get to the door. I chase after him, trying to block his path to the door but he scrambles around me. He's gone and Izzy stands there, crying and apologizing and our dad ushers us out to the car because we can't be late to school.

"You're such a bitch," I say to her through the rearview mirror.

"It's not her fault," Dad says. "She's not getting enough blood right now, she's so young."

I look at my sister, pale and shaking in the

backseat. Only two more weeks until I get paid.

At school, Kyle isn't waiting for me at my locker like usual. He walks by me in the hallways and looks over my head. People cross the hall when I pass. I fall asleep during my history test, and when it's over, I check my phone. A text from Bill: *we don't need you to come in for the rest of the week.*

At lunch, I sit alone. I scan the crowd of heads for Kyle. Try not to cry as I take out the mug of animal blood my dad packed me for lunch. As I drink, I try to study but the words in my textbook swirl in my brain. I touch my cheek to the cool pages of the book and close my eyes. I feel myself drifting when there's a squeak at the table and I look up to see Timmy, sitting in front of me with a thermos of blood, glowing red.

"I see you've finally decided to stop wasting your time on mortals." Timmy says.

"You're okay with not having any friends just because they're mortal?"

"They'll never understand us, Ava," Timmy says, swallowing a spoonful of blood, pinkening his lips. I look at him, cherry-mouthed and donned in a pristine collared shirt and expensive leather shoes. Next to him sits his name-brand backpack stuffed with fine-lined pens and his very own graphing calculator he doesn't have to rent from the school.

"What makes you think you understand me?" I ask.

"I know you have animal blood in your mug because your parents can't pay for Barry's shit anymore. He's really got a monopoly on the loose blood industry." I feel myself getting defensive, wanting to make up some lie so Timmy doesn't get any ideas about my family, but he knows he's right and I know I can't convince him otherwise.

"It tastes awful." I don't know why I feel like I can confide in him, but he's the only person who will get within ten feet of me. He answers with a soft, lopsided smile and slides his thermos over to me. I don't want to accept his handout, but my instincts kick in and soon I'm inhaling the blood, just like Izzy used to.

When I get home from school I go straight to my room. Izzy is already home, picked up early because she kept falling asleep in class. I sit in my room and play music in my headphones at the volume my mom often frowns at me for, telling me I'm going to damage my ears, and I have all eternity to live with blown out eardrums if I don't treat them well.

I take out my school books and lay them on the bed. I have so much homework to catch up on, and no job to get in the way of it. Kyle really screwed me over, but I still call him hoping he'll finally talk to me. Straight to voicemail.

I text him, tell him to call me, and put my phone aside. I have to get this work done. I open my precalculus textbook, and re-read the chapter, realizing I've only been half paying attention in class the past week. My mind drifts over the equations and my eyes pull shut.

When I wake up it's dark out and my phone is dead. I plug it in, anxious to see if Kyle has changed his mind about me. I sit there, waiting for the screen to light up, while my parents bicker downstairs. The phone screen turns on, lighting up my dark room. I rise at the sound of a notification.

I'll ask my dad if he has a job opening at the funeral home if you're interested. I toss my phone aside and join my parents in the kitchen.

"I want to go hunting with you guys tonight," I say.

"No," my mom says.

"Kyle broke up with me."

"We're not going hunting tonight," Dad says. Mom gives him a weird look.

"Why not?" I ask.

"I have other plans." I know it must be bad. They don't have enough money to get more loose blood, and unless there's some sort of loose blood black market I don't know about, the only other option is hunting mortals. But that can't be it. My dad wouldn't hurt anyone. I didn't think Izzy would either. Maybe all of us are capable of things we don't realize until we're desperate.

I pace back and forth in my room while I wonder who his victim will be. How will he choose who deserves to die? My dad, who would organize elaborate tea parties with my sister and I, my dad who cries at Disney movies, who brakes for squirrels, is going to kill someone? I sneak out of the house through my bedroom window.

Jacketless, I shiver in the cold as I walk through my neighborhood, on the way to Timmy's house. I imagine the refrigerator in his parents' kitchen being loaded with bags of blood. They probably waste blood all the time, and it doesn't matter to them like it matters to my family. I was starting to like Timmy and don't really want to steal from his family, but I can't ask him for what we need. I can't tell him why we need it.

I walk down the darkened streets towards the center of town, where the wealthier residents live. It's a nice night for December, the cold serving as an escape from the humidity typically plaguing the south, so there are a lot of people walking outside. Neighbors I know, some of whose kids I babysit from time to time, pass me by, giving gentle waves and smiles. In our neighborhood of sideways houses and broken-down cars, I feel closer to them than ever. A lot of the people here sell their blood to Barry's Blood Bank. I try not to dwell on the fact I've most likely consumed the blood of several of them.

I smile back at them, holding in tears. I realize I can smell each of them. Not in the normal way I usually smell humans, each with a different scent. Right now they all smell the same. The scent pulls me in. I smell their blood, crave it. I haven't eaten much all day, not even the meager offerings of animal blood from my parents, leaving me perpetually half-full. I'm starving, and after weeks without human blood it's the only thing I want. I veer off the sidewalk, away from the groups of neighbors, and walk three blocks away, down towards a clearing where an old house used to be but is currently a dried-up field of grass with a for sale sign on it. I sit in the grass and try to center myself, trying to remember these people are my neighbors. It feels like my body will take control and leap up, but I stop it. I hold myself firmly to the ground. I breathe in. I breathe out. In the distance I hear a rustle. A squirrel. I get up and rush to it, finding it scurrying towards a tree at the next property over. I grab it before it can get close, breaking its neck with the flick of my index finger. I've never killed anything before. It's easy.

I sink my teeth into its body and suck out the blood. My body settles, but I begin to cry. I hold the deflated corpse in my palms. I imagine holding my neighbor's baby like I am holding the squirrel. I drop it to the ground. I call Kyle, and there is an automated message saying he's unavailable. I know he's blocked me. I feel myself getting closer to losing control and I want to call my parents, but they don't know I left the house because I think in this case he might actually be the only person who understands, I call Timmy and ask him to pick me up. He pulls up less than ten minutes later in a shiny black Buick. He doesn't comment on my disheveled appearance or the squirrel corpse laying bloodied near my feet. I get into the passenger seat of his car and he hands me a glass water bottle filled with blood. I try to drink it at a respectable pace, but end up downing it before we get down the street.

"I asked my dad about a job for you by the way. He says they're looking for an intern," Timmy says when we pull into my neighborhood.

"How much does it pay?" I ask.

"I'm not sure. My dad's always saying something about how it pays in experience." He pulls up to my house and I'm hardly able to waste time feeling embarrassed as I see my parents getting into their car. They looked surprised to see me, especially with Timmy Morton.

"Where are you going?" I ask frantically. "Are you going hunting?"

"No," Dad says.

They don't let me ask any more questions, rolling up the window and backing out of the driveway.

The next morning, when Izzy and I join my parents in the kitchen they look tired, but light. On the table sit four helpings of blood, bright red and filled to the brim.

"Where's this from?" I ask, not daring to get too close to it, despite my body's desires.

"We caught a bear last night," Mom says. "Their blood is the best animal blood you can get." My parents sit down and look at me expectantly. I sit in front of my bowl of blood, not asking questions. We eat in silence.

A Raccoon Died at Fountain Park

At first, I couldn't comprehend it, because seeing a raccoon in the middle of the afternoon is like seeing a word you hardly know out of context. I tried to call my mom for the first time in two months, always assuming our lack of communication was on me to fix. I was leaving a voicemail trying not to sound too desperate, when I glanced up at the road and noticed it.

It looked at me—or, if I'm being honest, I wanted to believe it was looking at me. Its dark eyes blended into its masked face, making them impossible to discern. Then, it began drunkenly walking towards me. Well actually, calling it walking would be calling it something it wasn't, and I don't want to dishonor our time together.

What I will say is this: the raccoon placed its bony gray fists in front of itself, one after the other, and knuckle-dragged its body across the street, oblivious to the rough pavement peeling into its skin and scraping its stomach.

For a moment, I imagined grabbing its road-burned hand to help it find its way to the roaring fountain and wait out the end of its life. Sometimes, I thought I could be a person like that. Instead, I walked away.

Not wanting to miss my bus, I only retreated a little, behind a row of bushes, hoping it would leave me alone. I won't lie, I wanted the bus to arrive so that moment there with the raccoon would end. It looked pitiful and I couldn't muster care for another living thing. As I checked the bus schedule on my phone a rustle in the bushes pulled me from the screen. The raccoon's gray head emerged from the green and it looked up at me.

So, I ran. I ran to another bus stop in town, barely making it there in time. I got on the bus and went home. I texted my mom again, telling her about the raccoon, my quiet way of letting her know I missed her without giving her the space to pour water on my feelings. I moved on with my day.

It took a few weeks before I began to wonder about the raccoon, its coat so thin in my mind I could see its heaving ribcage, its chewed up ears. One time, when I was a kid, I was playing in the forest near our house when I saw one skittering through the trees. When I told my mom about it, she told me if you see a raccoon during the day it's rabid. Or maybe I read it somewhere. I'd always imagined rabies would turn you into some kind of half-human half-raccoon monster, making you lose all sense of yourself.

My raccoon hadn't looked like it could do anything terrible to me though. I spent hours one day typing a description of the creature I saw into Google, trying to find out what was wrong with it. The internet coughed up results about something called distemper, a fatal and debilitating disease.

Warning: Distempered raccoons face a decline in their mental state.

I wondered if the distempered raccoon had a family. Some days I imagined it was a mother— one of those really good ones who spent hours nuzzling through garbage to get her kids some green-fuzz covered orange peels, their favorite snack. I imagine it spent most of its life face-first in the intimate remains of people's lives, searching through their receipts and moldy food and tampons and pregnancy tests and college rejection letters.

I bet her kids didn't appreciate the work it took for her to bring them those peels, and they carried them back into the hole in the tree she hollowed out for them, forgetting to thank her. But my raccoon continued to care for her kids. I imagined her love for them was far-reaching, and lifelong, and gentle.

Warning: In the late stages of distemperment, raccoons lose their fear of humans. Raccoons with distemper may approach people or curl up to sleep in open areas.

I still imagine her here most frequently. I imagine I had known her distemperment, had known she was near death, had known she was a single mother. I would pick her large, bony body up off the road.

She would smell like garbage, but I wouldn't tell her. I would tell her she was going to be okay. She would lay motionless in my arms. I would carry her onto the sidewalk, down the trail leading to the fountain in the center of the park. I would ask if she could see the water. I would place her down as close to it as possible, letting the mist of the flipping fountain fall onto her fevered coat. My phone would buzz in my pocket. I would go to the nearest dumpster and find the raccoon orange peels with green fuzz. I would hold her bloody hand.

III.
Someone Better

Everyone Likes Taylor Swift

Taylor Swift comes to me in a forest during a melatonin-induced dream—skin made up of thousands of pieces of colored glass, glistening. I want to ask for an autograph for my wife, or when her next album is coming out, or why she only ever collaborates with male producers, but I notice she is crying. I'm no good at comforting crying people.

Tears slide down her cheeks, streaking the glass. I hand her a tissue and when she takes it, I notice her nails aren't painted, are short and shredded, are surrounded by inflamed skin.

"Are you okay?" I say, keeping my distance from her.

"Do you want to have a sleepover?" Taylor Swift

asks, as if we aren't both women in our thirties, far too old for air mattresses and all night long movie marathons. But what the hell, I think, this is Taylor Swift. I nod. She leads me deeper into the forest. The shade blankets us, but her reflective skin lights a path.

I follow, tripping over roots and feeling my hair frizz out from the humid air. We approach a wisteria tree, branches bent towards the ground, cascading lavender flowers. Taylor Swift parts the branches, takes my hand and pulls us through. The world shifts and we are hurled into a bedroom.

Surrounded by pale blue walls, I'm filled with an anger I'd forgotten. We are in my old bedroom, an oasis lit by the dim purple glow of lava lamps. Sixteen again. The walls are covered with photos of me and my high school best friend who kissed me once then pretended it never happened. The bony girls in blurry images laugh, and I can't tell if it's at us or with us. The pink carpet is blotted with nail polish stains. Taylor Swift twirls around, sparks spattering from her feet, as she takes in the bubblegum-scented time capsule of my life.

I paint Taylor Swift's nails sage with small gold flecks. When her nails dry, she braids my hair with pink ribbons and tells me the names of all the boys who broke her heart. I'm sixteen, so I make up a boy to love, I pretend her love songs make sense to me. I put glitter on her eyelids, and she teaches me how love is supposed to feel.

"Do you like my music?" Taylor Swift asks, her glass face glows purple under the light of the lamps. I laugh a little because I think she is joking, but I notice tears building in the corners of her eyes.

"I think everybody does, at least a little bit."

"But do you like it?" She leans in closer, places a glittering hand on my acne-spotted cheek.

The girls in school who like Taylor Swift are the same white girls who sit behind me in class or on the bus, throwing rolled up pieces of notebook paper at the back of my head to see how many will stick to my curls. I'm nothing like those girls. But I watch us grow older and heartbroken and more of my friends start listening to her music. On the first date with a woman who will become my wife, she tries hiding her Speak Now CD from me, ashamed of the frivolity of Taylor Swift's voice, those soft bells.

"I don't think we would've been friends in high school," I said, in my thirties again. Taylor Swift begins to cry and through tears and snot tells me she isn't surprised, nobody likes her. She cries so hard shards of glass slip off her face, revealing her perfect skin underneath. She fills my room with tears and more glass falls off her. It swirls around us in my aquarium, and we are flushed out of the window into my high school. Taylor Swift sits behind me and throws crumpled up paper balls into my frizzy brown hair.

Tent City

Amena is assembling sandwiches with lukewarm chicken patties, thinking about how disgusting it is that people still eat meat when Vlad, a fry cook who has a mullet and "mom" inside of a sunflower tattooed on his left bicep comes up behind her and says "are you coming to my party tonight?"

Vlad doesn't know Amena has a teenage daughter, doesn't know she is ten years older than him, doesn't know she was an up-and-coming journalist in the southeastern local news scene. Although to be fair, nobody under the age of forty pays much attention to the southeastern local news scene. Vlad pulls Amena in closer, "It's after the USC vs. Clemson game, so if the Gamecocks win you know it's gonna be a good party."

"I'll go if USC wins," Amena twirls her hair like she used to when she tried to flirt with boys when was younger. She knows she is a bad actor, but Vlad is too stupid to notice that Amena flirts with him just so he'll give her a milkshake with her comped meal even though employees are only allowed a fountain drink.

After six hours of twirling her hair and pretending to care about college football, Amena's shift is over. Vlad is putting together her usual meal: a spicy chicken sandwich, a large fry, and a peppermint Oreo milkshake. Amena watches as he scrawls his number on the side of the cup with a sharpie, the big blocky numbers covering up the Jack's Chicken Shack logo printed on the cup. She takes the food from him and pretends not to see the number, making it look like she absentmindedly smudged the marker with her thumb.

Amena brings the meal to Marv's usual spot at The Battery—the part of the harbor smelling of salty fish and dock workers—but Marv isn't there. Instead, there are a couple of workers drilling a new bar to his bench. Amena has seen this before— hostile architecture meant to keep people like Marv away from the eyes of tourists or rich locals who want to pretend Charleston is the perfect city.

"Excuse me," she says to a short man who is rifling through a box of bolts, "I was supposed to meet someone here, have you seen him? He has a long beard and is probably wearing this, like, gray hoodie that says San Francisco on it."

"The homeless dude? Yeah, the cops kicked him out of here this morning."

Amena walks the two blocks to Marv's best friend's camping spot, and Marv is there with Jack, who is packing up his few belongings.

"The cops are cracking down on us," Marv says, "We're moving to the underpass near the aquarium."

This happens every year around tourist season, and Amena sees the article she wrote for The Ashley Ridge Gazette didn't change anything. She hands Marv his meal and gives Jack a five-dollar bill from her wallet before heading home, hands twitching with anger.

Amena hangs her Jack's Chicken Shack visor on the hook next to the door once meant for her press passes and camera, and walks into the kitchen to see her daughter, Val, hunched over a four-inch binder bursting with loose leaf notebook paper and laminated handouts.

"Whatcha working on, strawberry head?" she ruffles her daughter's curly hair—Amena recently helped dye the left half of it pink with box dye—from behind. Val barely glances at Amena.

"Algebra," she huffs and scribbles something out. The eraser is already worn down on her pencil.

"I can't help you with math, I just work at the chicken shack." A smile breaks across Val's face and then falls before Amena can see it. Even though Amena tries to be a cool mom, she assumes Val, like all teenage daughters, thinks she is boring and old.

"How was work today?" Val pushes her incomplete work to the side. For some reason, Val began taking more of an interest in her mother after she was fired.

"Just as bad as always, but it pays the bills."

"That's capitalism," Val says. She had started reading Marx to impress her cousin who is a political science major at Winthrop, and is filled with one-liners about the woes of the establishment.

"What do you know about capitalism? You're fourteen."

"Mom, I'm not too young to know we're the proletariat. But at least you didn't let your boss take away your dignity."

"I'm a vegetarian who works at a chicken restaurant."

"But you feed gross, capitalist chicken to an unhoused guy."

Amena laughs. She is never not amazed at how intense her daughter is in her first year of high school. Amena was nowhere near as opinionated as her when she was fourteen. She wasn't even opinionated when she was sixteen, taking care of Val full time, and fighting the welfare office to keep her on the WIC program.

"Did you see Marv today?" Val asks, erasing another failed equation.

"Yeah, they're all moving though. City is adding bars on the benches and cracking down on people camping on street corners."

"They put bars on the benches?"

"We were always getting emails from locals telling us to write about them."

"Why didn't you?"

"Larry said it was too controversial."

"Fuck Larry."

"Hey, language," she tries to give her daughter a stern look, but Amena is sure Val can sense the smile hiding behind her closed lips.

The next day, Amena is cooking beans, thinking about how much she misses vegetarian meat but can't afford it on her Chicken Shack salary, when Val and her best friend Tyrell walk into the house. Val sniffs once and makes a face.

"Beans again, mom?" Val drops her backpack on the ground and rolls her eyes.

"Tyrell, I'm making burritos if you want to stay for dinner."

"Thanks, Ms. Morales."

"Tyrell, if you keep calling me that old lady name you won't be allowed to date my daughter anymore."

Tyrell mocks fear. "How will I ever live without her," he wraps his arms around Val's shoulders and the two erupt with laughter. Val and Tyrell pretend to date so Tyrell's Christian parents stop trying to set their closeted gay son up with petite and proper girls who are youth group members at the megachurch in town.

"After dinner, we're going to the movies at the discount theater, is that okay?" Val asks.

"Which movie?"

"Ah, I don't know some nerdy thing Tyrell picked out."

"You leave him alone. Grab ten dollars from my purse." Amena can't shake the habit of giving her daughter money whenever she asks, despite ten dollars being a much bigger deal to her now than it had been when she still had her job at the paper.

"Thanks mom," Val kisses her cheek and she and Tyrell go up to her room and blast some new album they won't stop listening to until dinner is ready.

After Val and Tyrell leave, Amena spends the evening watching reruns of *Keeping Up with the Kardashians*, yelling at the TV about how stupid everyone is and eating waffles with syrup and sugar poured on top of them. She doesn't spend time with her friends anymore because she can't bear to have them ask her how she's doing with pitiful looks in their eyes. After a few episodes, Amena realizes Val hasn't come home yet and tries calling her, getting sent to voicemail. She gets into her car and drives around, stopping at the theater and the Waffle House next door, and eventually all the way to The Battery.

She walks the perimeter of the park, calling their names. Streetlamps line the waterfront, but the rest of the park is dark, Amena can barely make out the silhouette of the Angel Oak tree and the confederate monuments lining the greenery.

Amena keeps walking, and as she reaches the smelly part of the harbor she sees Val in the distance, hunched over Marv's old bench, with Tyrell holding his phone flashlight. As she gets closer, she sees Val is holding a wrench, twisting the bolt holding in the bench's bar.

"Val? Stop!" Amena yells and Tyrell dives to the ground. Val drops the wrench, and it hits her foot. She looks up with wide eyes until she realizes it is her mother.

"Mom, how'd you find us?"

Tyrell is still on the ground, visibly shaken.

"You know this is illegal, right? And you dragged poor Tyrell into this. Do you know how much trouble you could've gotten into?"

"It's not right how they treat them."

"You're breaking the law." Amena picks the wrench up off the ground. It still has a price tag on it.

"I told you we shouldn't—" Tyrell stammers from his spot on the ground.

"Shut up Tyrell. We're just trying to help people."

"There are better ways to help people," Amena says.

"You always say you want to help them but giving them food in secret isn't going to help anybody. Me and Tyrell are actually doing something. You got fired for nothing."

"We're going home. Now."

Amena throws their bikes in her trunk and brings Tyrell home. He looks like he is going to hurl in the backseat until she tells him she won't tell his parents what they did. When they arrive at home Val goes to her room and slams the door.

The next day, Amena drops Val off at school on her way to her opening shift at Jack's Chicken Shack. Val sits in the front seat with her headphones in, music so loud Amena can hear it.

As soon as Amena gets to work, Vlad finds her and starts asking her why she wasn't at his party the night before. He is ten minutes into a soliloquy about getting hammered off six Miller Lites when Amena can't take it anymore.

"I wasn't at your party last night because my daughter was being a brat."

"Wait, so you're a mom?" Vlad backs up from Amena, giving her space for the first time since they worked together. "I thought you went to USC?"

"Nope. And I'm a vegetarian."

Vlad is about to respond but turns around and runs to the bathroom instead. He lies to the boss and tells him it is the stomach flu, not a hangover, and is sent home.

"Amena, I need you to be on the fryer until we can get a replacement for Vlad."

"You want me to cook the chicken? Sir I can't—"

"You just put it in the fryer, it's not rocket science. There's a book of instructions on my desk you can look over. We need to have 100 patties by opening time."

Amena reads over the instructions and her boss is right, it is simple. She adds oil to the fryer and turns it on, throwing in a few patties at a time. Grease splashes up and lands on her face, hair, and clothes. As she cooks patties, accumulating a thin layer of grease all over her body—she is starting to understand why Vlad has such bad acne—she keeps thinking about how many chickens had to die to make all this food. She misses her old job and her air-conditioned office and never having to contribute to this particular blight on society.

Ten minutes before opening she is saved by Sam; the evening shift cook who had the misfortune of picking up the phone when their boss called. Amena is put back on register duty, and welcomes the break from staring at dead chickens.

Amena puts on her customer service voice when a woman comes in and orders a chicken sandwich with mustard and no pickles. She cashes her out and hands her the food once the cook packs it up. The woman takes the food and leaves with a smile. There's no line so Amena tries to pass time by wiping down the counters, and when it finally is as clean as it can get the woman walks back in, the unwrapped sandwich in her hand.

"I specifically said no pickles." She waves the sandwich in Amena's face, mustard dripping down onto her hands.

"I'm sorry can I—"

"And yet I took a bite of my sandwich and bit into this," the woman pulls a pickle, covered in mustard, out of her sandwich and smacks it down onto the freshly cleaned countertop, splashing mustard on Amena's uniform.

"Ma'am I can—"

"Let me speak to your manager." Amena calls the manager over, who gives the women a free meal and Amena goes back to the register to help the next customer She tries not to be embarrassed by the mustard stain on her shirt.

"Welcome to Jack's, what can I get for you today?" She looks up and it takes her a moment to realize she is looking at her asshole-ex-boss, Larry. He looks at Amena in her bright blue visor, mustard smeared on her shirt.

"Aren't you a vegetarian?"

"What can I get for you?"

"Do you want your job back?"

"Would you like to try our seasonal peppermint milkshake?"

"Seriously, I hate seeing you work here. You can have your job back, you just have to be less political. Also, that milkshake sounds great. And a number two please."

Larry hates homeless people. But Larry would never admit it. Larry would tell you the reason he fired Amena is because it was "totally unethical" for her to buy food for sources, after she interviewed Marv for an article about Charleston's housing crisis and subsequently bought him groceries each week.

"You'd really give me my job back?"

"I mean, I'd probably have to start you off on a different beat to avoid the mess from before and we'd have to have a talk about ethics but, yeah. You're a good worker."

Amena doesn't understand how she is expected to spend weeks interviewing a man who needs help without helping him and then go home and eat expensive vegetarian meals with her daughter. Larry thinks the best way to help Marv is to affect change through journalism. Weeks ago, Amena told him she thought that was fucking stupid and so now every day she puts on a blue polo and matching visor to serve chicken corpses on buns to customers who throw pickles at her for eight hours a day.

"$9.25."

Larry hands Amena a twenty-dollar bill. "Will

you think about it?"

"I'll think about it." She hands him his receipt.

At the end of her shift, Sam gives Amena her comped meal, no milkshake. Amena knows Marv will be disappointed, but she goes down to The Battery to find him anyway. She can't figure out how to get to the underpass where he said he was staying, so she parks her car at the aquarium and walks. As she approaches the underpass, she notices it is lined with dozens of faded tents. Men, women, and children in tattered clothes sit in groups around makeshift bonfires. There are two men with long beards sharing a tallboy and playing cards. A teenage boy walks up to her with a cracked solo cup filled with quarters. Amena puts a five-dollar bill in his cup and he hugs her.

"Do you know Marv?" She asks, "I think he's staying here."

"He and Jack stay together over there," he points to a light blue tent about twenty feet away from the others, "Jack doesn't like being around us much."

"That sounds like Jack. Thank you."

Amena approaches the tent and peeks into the open flap to find Marv alone, scribbling away at a paper.

"Hey Marv," She hands him the greasy bag.

"Thanks Amena."

"This is quite the community going on down here."

"Ah yeah, Jack can't stand 'em. He keeps talking about how he might just go sit on the spikes they put on his street corner to put himself out of his misery."

Amena thinks writing about tent city could be a great first story if she takes her job back, but then she remembers what Larry said about putting her on a different beat. And she remembers she wouldn't be able to be friends with Marv and Jack anymore if she wrote about Tent City. She sits in silence with Marv as he writes, thinking about what she will say to Larry about his offer.

When Amena gets home, Val is practicing flashcards for her biology class at the kitchen table.

"Hey Val, guess what? Larry came into the shack today and told me I could have my job back." Amena can almost taste the Wednesday night margaritas she'd get with her coworkers and smell the ink on freshly printed newspapers.

"And you told him no, right?" This is one of the first things Val has said to Amena since she grounded her.

"I was thinking about telling him yes."

"Because you don't actually care about Marv and Jack." Val grabs her flashcards and goes upstairs to her room.

That night, Amena fills a glass of wine to the brim and begins writing a pros and cons list of going back to her old job.

Pro: she could help all the people in Tent City more than just giving Marv a lukewarm chicken sandwich every day. Pro: she could afford better things for Val. Con: Larry won't let her have opinions. Pro: she'd get her dignity back. Con: what good is dignity if she didn't have her morals?

Amena crumbles up the paper and finishes her glass of wine. She turns on the television and flips through channels hoping something interesting will be on. She mutes the television when she hears a banging noise from Val's room.

"Val?" No answer. Amena runs upstairs and opens the door to her bedroom to find Val leaning out of her open window, attaching the fire escape ladder they keep in the house to her bedroom window. "What are you doing?"

Val jumps and the ladder slips out of her hands, landing with a loud thud on the grass below. Then there's a scream. Tyrell.

Amena leans out the window, "Ty, get in here." Tyrell picks up the ladder and walks around to the front door.

"I need to do something, Mom."

Tyrell comes into the room and hands Amena the ladder. "Sorry Ms. Morales."

"Come on, let's get in the car." Val sighs and places the toolbox she is holding on her bed. "Bring that with you," Amena says.

She drives them down to The Battery and they find the benches with freshly added bars. "Show me how it's done," Amena says. Tyrell is on lookout while Val shows Amena where the bolts are and how to remove them.

"It's really easy to remove them since they were added on as an afterthought," Val hands her mom the wrench to undo the other bolt. "Although Ty and I never really decided what we'd do with the bar once we got it off."

Amena holds the bar in her hand and looks around for a good place to put it. She pulls her arm all the way back and then throws the bar into the harbor. The three spend the rest of the night slinking through the dark Charleston streets, ripping bars off of benches and throwing them into the ocean. Amena can't wait to tell Marv and Jack what they had done. For the first time in her life, Amena feels like she is doing something real and tangible, not just words on a page.

The three sleep in past noon the next day, but as soon as they wake up Amena drives them back into downtown so they can share the news with the people of Tent City. As they make their way under the overpass, they hear the static of walkie-talkies and see red and blue flashing lights under the bridge. As Tent City comes into view, they see droves of cops cuffing the residents of the makeshift city. There is trash on the ground, and the cops are breaking the already worn-down tents and throwing them into large garbage bags. Amena stops walking, Tyrell and Val stop shortly behind her. At Amena's feet is a cracked red solo cup.

Apparition of The Virgin Mary in a McDonald's Drive-Thru

As I drop my heavy body into the front seat of my car after a ten-hour shift and look in the rearview mirror to see The Virgin Mary sitting in the back, I am a little shocked, but mostly annoyed I have something new to deal with when all I want is something to eat.

"We're going to McDonald's," I tell her as I start the car, not giving her room to explain herself to me. She sits in the back seat of my blue Honda Civic, feet surrounded by all the stuff I've collected in my car but never bothered to clean out: dirty sweatshirts, empty Pepsi bottles, an ice scraper, a half empty box of tampons in case of emergencies, and more receipts than I can count.

"Who is McDonald?" she asks. As the engine gears up, Mary startles and stares at the lights flashing on the dash.

"Not everyone can afford to take their car to the dealership every time the check engine light comes on, okay?"

Mary doesn't respond. Instead, she sits there, twisting a loose thread on her blue robes between her thumb and forefinger. I begin to pull the car out of my parking spot, its light illuminating the mostly dark sixth level of the parking garage reserved for the janitors and maintenance staff at the hospital—all the low-level employees that management doesn't care about. To them, it doesn' matter if we get murdered in the poorly lit space.

Mary moves away from the window to the middle seat, pulling her knees to her chest, breathing hard.

"Woah, what's up with you?" I say, glancing back at her in my rearview mirror. Her face is even whiter than how all the paintings and statues in my parents' church depict her. I realize Mary has never been in a car before.

I park in the middle of the lot and lean back to help Mary with her seat belt. For maybe the first time ever, I am glad I work the graveyard shift because nobody is around to ask questions about the woman in my car. Mary flinches as I try buckling her in.

"Just trust me, okay?" She settles a bit. I pull the belt over her waist and click it in, suddenly feeling silly. Surely

The Virgin Mary is immortal. "Are you hungry?" I ask. She nods.

I hesitate before starting the car back up. I'm not sure how to explain all of this to Mary, especially when I'm covered in sweat and half asleep.

"This is a car," I say. She doesn't respond. I'm pretty sure they rode donkeys to Jerusalem from what I remember from my Catholic school days. "It's kinda like a donkey, but louder. And with lights." Mary nods knowingly, which makes me think I'm right about the donkey thing.

On the drive to McDonald's, I try pointing things out to Mary, but how do you explain gas stations or streetlights or traffic to someone who never had basic electricity? So instead, I sit in the front seat, reaching for something we might have in common.

"You know, my parents are real Jesus freaks," I say.

"One who worships the Lord is nary a freak." The word freak fills her mouth like tar.

"Jesus doesn't help people like they say he does," I say, itching my thigh through my stiff polyester pants. I hate this stupid uniform. I hate working the night shift, driving home when my eyes can barely remain open. I've gotta get a new job. I blink hard and continue to drive.

"All who live in the Kingdom of God shall be blessed by him. He looks after his children," Mary says, startling me out of my internal monologue.

I like quiet car rides. My commute is the only time I don't have to report to a boss or listen to my roommates drone on about how we need more paper towels. But now, for some unknown reason, The Virgin Mary is in my car ruining the only blissful part of my day.

"If I was really living in God's kingdom, I don't think my job would be cleaning up people's shit in a hospital bathroom," I respond. I have a moment of remorse, thinking I should probably be less crass, but my stomach rumbles again. I think of the Big Mac I am ready to shove in my mouth. Which is a basic human need. You can't blame me for trying to fulfill that before I figure out what the fuck I'm meant to do with the patron saint who wound up in my back seat.

"You don't like your vocation?" Mary asks.

"Does anyone?"

"Does it provide you with the means to live?" she asks.

"Hardly. But I make do."

"Do you provide for your family?"

"I don't have a family. Just me and my cat, Banjo."

"You live with a cat?" She looks disgusted. "Cats belong outside."

"Not Banjo. He's high maintenance."

"A woman your age should be taking care of a family, not a cat" she says.

"You sound just like my mother." Between me, her gay child, and my sister, her barren child, my mother loves to complain about how she'll never have grandkids. But at least my sister only has a biological failing, rather than a moral failing. I think about telling Mary this just to see if all the bullshit the priest at my parents' church spews is true, but I

140

decide I can't take finding out whether The Virgin Mary is homophobic at 3AM.

"They call me the patron saint of motherly care for a reason," she laughs. I almost laugh too, but it's pretty gauche of her to refer to herself as a patron saint.

I have the sudden suspicion Mary can read my mind. She's Jesus' fricking mother after all. And the priest of my parents' church told us Jesus is always watching.

Jesus watches you when you lie. Jesus watches you when you're kind. Jesus watches you when you shit. Jesus watches you when you pray. Jesus watches you when you have sex with a girl for the first time at bible camp in the tenth grade.

"Goddamnit, The Virgin Mary knows I am thinking about lesbian sex. Goddamnit, The Virgin Mary just heard me think Goddamnit and I'm pretty sure that goes against the Ten Commandments or whatever.

I peer into my rearview mirror to see if she is reacting to all the lewd thoughts occurring in my mind on repeat—because once you think of fucking a woman when you're not supposed to, your brain thinks about it exponentially harder the more you try not to think about it—but she sits there, seemingly unphased, staring out the window at the shopping mall we are driving past. I think about how Mary has never witnessed the ravenous pillage of shoppers on a Saturday night. All she's seen of it— and maybe all she will ever see of it—is a dark looming building and an empty parking lot, except for two cars which I assume belong to janitors. I feel solidarity with them for a moment.

"Mary?"

"Yes, my child?" It takes all of my will to not roll my eyes.

"Can you like, read my mind?" I ask, looking to see her response, to gauge whether she'll lie to me. But of course, she won't lie to me, she's The Virgin Mary. Born pure of sin. A perfect daughter and a perfect woman from the very beginning. I wonder what that's like.

"What an absurd question. Of course I cannot see into your thoughts. I am no witch," she scoffs.

"Geez, okay, pretend I never asked."

"Pretending is lying."

"Sorry. We're getting close, what do you want to eat?" I ask.

"Whatever you deign to give me. Beggars shall not be choosers," she responds.

"Well one of the great things about McDonald's is they let you pick. And we aren't beggars, we are paying them money."

"This McDonald is a very generous man."

"Not a man."

"Oh. A woman then?"

"Not a woman. A corporation."

"Cor-por-a-tion?"

"It's a big rich company who owns a bunch of restaurants and pays people low wages to work for them."

"What work does the corporation do? Why do they get all the money?"

"I'm not sure. I don't think they do much except maybe make spreadsheets all day."

"So, they are textile workers? Textile workers are valuable to their communities."

"Spreadsheets are like something you do on a computer. I don't have time to explain this to you, Mary. We're almost there."

"Hmmm."

"What do you want to eat?" I see the golden arches lighting up the navy night sky. She needs to choose quickly. Nothing is more nerve wracking than pulling up to a drive-thru window without a clear order set in my mind.

"Perhaps some fish?" She can barely get the words out, as though she's never made a decision on her own before.

"I can get you a Filet-O-Fish. It's like a fish sandwich."

"Sandwich?"

"It's like, two pieces of bread with meat in the middle. Probably one of the world's greatest foods. Although the Filet-O-Fish isn't a great sandwich."

"Bread and fish. Okay."

"I'm gonna get a McFlurry too," I say, turning into the McDonald's parking lot, "you want one?" She stares blankly. "Right. You don't know what a McFlurry is. Do you know what ice is?" I pull into the line.

"Sometimes, if there was a chill in the air, ice would appear on trees." Mary says.

"Yeah, so like ice, but a whole bunch of it in a cup and you can eat it."

"You eat ice?"

"It's more than ice. It's like frozen milk I guess?"

"You take the ice from trees?" she asks.

"There are ice making machines now. And it keeps everything cold. Like a really cold box." She nods. "So, a McFlurry is made of ice and milk. And there's M&Ms in it."

Her mouth forms a thin line.

"M&Ms are colorful chocolate candies."

"I have never had chocolate, but I have heard marvelous tales of it from the New World," she says. "Why is it not brown?"

"They dye it in a factory or some shit. I don't know everything," I say. There is only one car left in front of me. "Do you want one or not?" I feel my voice raising and try to clamp it down. I will not yell at The Virgin Mary. I will not yell at The Virgin Mary. I will not yell at The Virgin Mary. "It's almost our turn to order."

"I am not sure if this McFlurry will be good for me," she says. "Does it hurt?"

"Why would it hurt?"

"Sometimes, when it snowed in Jerusalem, we were not expecting the weather and didn't take the donkeys in. They would sometimes freeze to death. If I eat this frozen milk-ice concoction, will I freeze to death?" God, she is getting on my nerves. I pull up to the speaker. It is our turn to order.

"No, it's not going to make you freeze to death. Do you want the McFlurry or not?"

"Hi, Welcome to McDonald's! How can I help you?" the voice of a barely pubescent boy cracks out of the speaker. I look back at Mary, her face lit up by the yellow glow of the drive-thru menu, eyes wide.

"Uhhh, can I help you?" the voice sounds again. I look at Mary in anticipation. I scratch my thigh as I wait for her to give me a response.

"I need just one moment. So sorry," I say. I swear I hear the kid sigh.

"Sure, no problem."

"Mary. Make a decision. Right now," I say. She squints against the fluorescent lights.

"I suppose I will take your frozen milk," she says, and continues to stare out the window.

"Sorry about the delay. We're ready to order now," I say to the speaker.

"What can I get for you?" the voice says.

"Can I get a medium Big Mac meal with a Diet Coke, and a medium Filet-O-Fish meal," I hesitate and almost ask Mary what she wants to drink, but decide not to, "also with a Diet Coke."

"Sure thing," the speaker says. "Anything else?'

"Can I get two small M&M McFlurries please." There is silence. Then a crackle. I hear the boy breathing again.

"I'm sorry ma'am, our ice cream machine is broken at the moment."

Goddamnit.

"Thank you so much, then. That will be all."

"Your total is $10.87, pull up to the second window." The speaker goes silent.

"No McFlurry, Mary," I say. She looks disappointed. "Their damn ice cream machine hardly ever works." I can tell she wants to ask about the ice cream machine, but she doesn't, and I don't attempt to explain. I pull up to the second window, and it takes less than a minute for a boy with blonde hair and severe cystic acne to pop out of it with our food in hand. I pay, thank him, and drive off.

"That young boy is much like the Lord. For he has filled the hungry with good things but has sent the rich away empty." Mary says, taking the greasy Filet-O-Fish package from me.

"They definitely don't turn away the rich. Nobody does. Not even churches. They love the rich."

"They should love the rich, because they should love all of God's children equally." She unwraps the sandwich and brings it to her nose, inhaling deeply.

"I wouldn't say it's very equal."

Mary takes a small bite out of the corner of the sandwich and frowns.

"It burned my mouth," she says.

"You could blow on it to cool it down." I say. "Like this," I purse my lips and blow air out of them. She mimics me. Then, after a moment, she tries to take another bite.

"That is," she begins, taking another bite, "delicious."

"I told you, sandwiches rock." I pass her soda back to her. She takes a sip and giggles when the fizz roars up her throat, spitting a bit of it out. I laugh along with her, not thinking about how I'll have to clean up its sticky residue later. I wish I could give her a McFlurry to try.

"I am quite fond of you," she says, taking another sip of soda. "You are a very impressive young woman.

Likely a great mother to Banjo. Tell me more about him."

"He's fourteen years old. He's orange. He eats all my plants."

"Bad cat," she says. I nod.

"I love him anyways," I say.

"Why?"

"He's just always been there for me. The world feels cozier when I come home to him." For some reason I want to tell her things.

"How lovely. It sounds like you really believe in him."

"Mary, why did you come here?" I ask.

"I am not sure. I suppose God sent me."

"I don't understand why he'd send you to me. I'm not the kind of person he'd like too much," I say.

"God loves all of his children."

"Sure. Heard that before."

"Of course you have. Such is the truth."

"Mary, where am I supposed to take you?" I look at her again through the rearview mirror, smiling at how her cheeks shine with grease.

"Let me come home with you. I want to meet this cat of yours," she says. I consider fighting it, partially because I want to go home and sleep, but mostly because I don't want The Virgin Mary to see the state of my small dingy apartment I share with two other people, but I don't want this night to end yet. I nod at her and continue to drive. We continue the drive in near silence, the symphony of our chewing filling the car, disturbed only by the occasional question from Mary, each of which I try to answer in as few words as possible. I'm tired of explaining things.

Eventually, she stops asking questions. We finish the dark drive in silence, and it's kind of nice to have her here. I think about the pile of laundry I left on the couch before I came into work. And the dishes my roommate probably left in the sink. My apartment is not fit for Jesus' mother, but I suppose there's nothing I can do now. She is going to see all of it, and I don't mind. After five minutes of silence, I pull into the parking lot.

"This is it, Mary," I say. I hear a small thud. I turn around to invite her in, but the backseat is empty. Mary is gone. I didn't get the chance to say goodbye. I would've thought I imagined the whole thing if it wasn't for the mostly eaten Filet-O-Fish sitting atop a crumpled wrapper remaining where she had been sitting. I reach into the back seat and pick up the wrapper, along with the other trash piled up back there for months and throw it away once I'm inside my apartment.

Peanut Butter

Peanut Butter the betta fish's corpse floating at the top of his bowl lets me know my wife plans on killing me next. His limp blue body is a warning, a proverbial head on a stake. I pick up Peanut Butter's bowl, cradle it into my chest, and bring it to the bathroom. I place the bowl on the counter and stare into his glazed over black eyes. Using a q-tip from the top drawer, I poke his body.

I only fucked my coworker one time.

I poke Peanut Butter again. This time a scale falls off, floats to the bottom of the bowl and sinks into the pink rocks at the bottom. I sniff the water to see if she poisoned him. It smells like fish. I check his box of food to see if she overfed him. The box is full. I don't know how she killed him but staring at his slimy skin is getting to me. I dump Peanut Butter into the toilet, along with all the water, the pebbles, and even the tiny castle Emma bought for him on the way home from the fair where we won him while playing ring toss.

"See ya later, Peanut." I flush the toilet. The gray plastic castle won't fit. It just keeps banging against the side of the bowl. Water splashes up, getting on my shirt and chin.

"What are you doing down there?" Emma is quiet when she walks, so I don't hear her coming. "Is Peanut Butter dead?" She puts a freshly manicured hand up to her mouth, faking shock at what she's done. I don't respond, just try to flush the toilet again. Emma peers over the bowl and water splashes us both.

"Are you trying to flush his castle?" She plunges her hand into the toilet water, not minding her manicure. She scoops it up and drops it into the sink. "What happened to him?" The edges of her eyes pool over with tears. It is pathetic to watch.

"I don't know, he's your fish" I stand up, careful to avoid slipping on toilet water.

"Real nice, Olivia." She pumps soap into her hands and starts scrubbing, steam jumps up from the water as it gains heat. "He was fine this morning." She keeps scrubbing.

We've had Peanut Butter for almost a year. Emma won him at the state fair on our two-year wedding anniversary. Emma named him Peanut Butter because I had walked around with peanut butter smudged on my face for most of the night before either of us noticed. We finally noticed when we took photos in a photo booth. The photo still hangs on the fridge with a magnet we bought from a cheesy gift shop during a trip to Atlanta the year before.

I walk over to the sink and turn off the water,

then rip the turquoise towel from the shelf and hand it to her.

"I just really loved him." She wipes her hands dry and leaves the bathroom, grabbing the plastic castle on the way out.

My glasses sit high up on my nose as I squint at the pink stitches I crocheted together, trying to figure out where I'm meant to put the hook next. Emma showed me how to do it a few weeks ago and she made it look so easy. But she does have an effortless way about her. She gets dressed in ten minutes each morning, goes on runs without breaking a sweat, and rises through the ranks in her firm without ever once getting stressed out. Meanwhile, I still can't pass the bar.

"Babe, if you stare any closer, you're going to poke your eye out with your hook," Emma says, startling me so much I almost do.

"That's what the glasses are for. Protection." I tap my lens with the hook. She laughs. I continue my attempt at shoving the hook into a stitch it probably doesn't belong in.

"Wanna go to Chipotle for lunch tomorrow? I've been craving a rice bowl," Emma asks as she settles into the couch, working on a sweater for her mom.

"I can't, I have a meeting with one of the new hires."

"Is it with Madison?" she asks, "how's she been doing? I know y'all were hesitant to hire her."

My hook slips out of my hand, landing on the

ground with a deafening clink. I look up at her to see if she is staring me down, to see if I can feel the suspicion coming off her, but she is focused on sewing in the ends of one of the sweater sleeves. She doesn't flinch when the hook hits the floor.

"It's with Tyler."

"Madison is doing well then?" She says this to her sweater more than me.

"She's doing fine, I guess. I don't work with her very often."

"But you're the manager?"

I bend down to pick the fallen hook up off the ground. "Yes. But we have a very hands-off relationship."

"I suppose being a Rite Aid manager isn't the most hands-on job in the world." Emma continues to crochet. The hook slips past my fingertips and rolls under the chair she is sitting in. She doesn't offer to help me as I sit at her feet and stick my hand beneath the furniture searching for the cool touch of the metal hook.

For the rest of the week, I walk around our house on high alert. I take the bus to work each day to ensure Emma won't get me by cutting the brakes on my car. Each night I lay in bed awake, monitoring her movement. I had forgotten how loudly she snores.

On Sunday morning, I wake up early, looking for clues of what she has planned for me. Emma passed out when she donated blood once, so I'm not expecting to find anything as obvious as a gun or knife. Maybe I'll find the poison she fed our fish.

Emma sleeps, snoring like a lawn mower the entire time I search through her dresser drawers. I find a lot of tops she borrowed from me and never returned, but nothing more incriminating. By the time Emma wakes, rubbing her tiny brown fists into her tired eyes, a gesture once so endearing to me before I had to start wondering what those fists were capable of, I have searched every inch of our home and am not any closer to figuring out the way she intends to end my life.

"Hey, can you cut my hair today? It's getting out of hand," Emma gestures to her hair, much longer than the usual bob she keeps to seem polished while in court, sticking out at every end and tangled from her long stint in bed. I say yes, almost forgetting about how she wants me dead. This has been a monthly tradition since we were both in law school, too poor to go to a salon. Even though she can afford salon cuts now, Emma always claims to like mine better.

I white-knuckle the shearing scissors close to my wife's scalp, hyper-aware of my control over her life. As I cut layers into her almond hair, pieces of her fall to the ground.

"Don't forget to angle it towards my face, hun. Otherwise, it looks boxy."

She reminds me every time as if I'll forget any detail of her. I grab the front part of her hair and twist it, preparing for the cut. As I bring my scissors close to her face, I think about how angling her hair gives me the perfect opportunity to go for it. If I slip a little to the left, I can land the point of the scissors right into her eye. I'd have to push hard if I want her dead fast. I've read the temple is instant, too, if you stab it hard enough. But blood will get everywhere. Blood is a pain in the ass to clean up. And I think we're out of bleach.

Emma grabs my hand with the scissors, mid cut.

"Don't go too short." She tries to pull the scissors from my hand, but I tighten my grip.

"Sorry." I put the shearing scissors down. Out of her reach. I run the comb through her hair, "All done."

She kisses me on the temple, leaving cherry red gloss on my head.

When Emma leaves the room, I throw on some leggings and my sneakers to go out for a run.

I burst out of our front door into the crisp air already in a light jog, eager to put some distance between myself and our house. As my green shoes slap the pavement of our subdivision, I try to drown out the thoughts of my wife, likely scheming against me. I wonder if I should say something to her. Tell her how sorry I am for sleeping with Madison. I'll tell her Madison came onto me.

As I approach the second mile of my run, sweat builds up on the back of my neck and on the inside of my knees and I keep thinking about Madison. I don't want to think about Madison laying me down on the still-damp freshly mopped floor and her disinfectant-covered hands finding their way into my pants, but it is impossible. Fucking her is uncomplicated.

I get back from my run, kick my shoes off at the front door and listen for Emma. I hear the shower running and feel a sense of relief knowing she is in a more vulnerable position than I am. I go into the kitchen to make a protein shake. As I reach into the back of the refrigerator to grab the container of blueberries, I accidentally grab the container of grape tomatoes—which Emma buys just for my salads, since she's allergic.

Instead of replacing the tomatoes in the refrigerator I grab them and the berries and bring them to the counter. I grab the rest of the ingredients and throw them in the blender. Then I slice up two grape tomatoes into thin disks, squirting red juice on the countertop, and add them in.

I begin blending the ingredients, making sure the purple of the berries and the white of the yogurt mask the color of the tomatoes.

"Hey Emma," I call up the staircase, "I made you something."

No response. I stand there for five minutes with the smoothie glass in my hand, sweating onto my palm. Finally, I hear a light patter coming down the stairs. When she rounds the corner, I slide one glass across the table to her and take a gulp out of mine. I can't taste the tomatoes.

She looks at the smoothie, then looks up at me. Her face is pale.

"Do I feel hot?" She walks towards me, tilting her head up at me. I place my hand on her head. It feels like picking a pan out of the oven without a mitt. I feign concern, and she sees it on my face. "Oh no, hold on," she runs to the bathroom, and I can hear her retching. I gulp down the rest of my smoothie. The closer I get to the bottom the more it tastes like ketchup.

I hear Emma continue to throw up and figure I should check on her. She looks helpless as she hunches over the toilet, the back of her neck glistening with sweat. I hand her a towel.

I half carry her up the stairs to our room and once she is tucked under the covers I go to the kitchen and make a cup of tea, grab a bottle of Advil, and bring them upstairs. I place the tea and Advil on the bedside table. Emma is curled up in the corner of our bed, already asleep.

I sleep on the couch while my wife snores in our room. I hear her get out of bed every hour or so to dry heave into the toilet. Every time she moves, I tense up. Maybe this is a trick. As I finally drift off to sleep at almost 4 AM I hear slow footsteps coming down the stairs. I leap up on the couch so fast Emma grips the handrail to avoid losing her footing.

"Sorry I scared you," her voice croaks.

"What are you doing down here?" I look to see if she is holding anything in her hand, but it's too dark to be sure.

"I came down to make some tea."

"I can make it for you."

"You should get some sleep."

I don't fight her because I am so tired. I stay on the couch, trying to stay awake until she is back in our room, but after what feels like only a second, I am reopening my eyes to Emma looming above me. I hear a faint tap and then she vanishes. I look to see a cup of tea placed on the coffee table next to my head.

As soon as she is gone and I can work up the energy to stand, I dump the tea into the sink.

In the morning I go upstairs to check on my wife and keep an eye on her. When I get to our room and open the door, she is merely a bump on the bed with her curly hair poking out the top of the blanket. Her snoring is louder than usual.

I place a glass of orange juice on the bedside table and catch a glimpse of her face, still as she sleeps. It is the first time in a while I haven't feared my wife.

Emma opens one eye slightly, "Hey."

"How are you feeling?"

"A little better. Will you stay with me for a while?"

I nod and sit in the armchair in the corner of our room. Emma turns on the light next to the bed and grabs a book from the nightstand. I resume my crooked attempt at crochet. We sit in silence except for the occasional cough from Emma, riling me up out of my chair each time. I know it could be simple. Break the carbon monoxide detector and leave the stove on when I leave for work. Or circle back to the previous plan and slip some tomatoes in something I make for her. I could shoot her in her sleep.

With each stitch of the blanket, I think about what my next move will be. I need to protect myself. I want to figure out how she figured it out. Emma keeps reading, occasionally laughing from her nose and reciting a line. She looks healthier today and it makes me wonder if she is faking it. I look at the blanket, messy and uneven, stitches popping out of the sides and know while it would make a horrible blanket, it could be a perfect tool to kill Emma. Nobody would suspect a yarn-monstrosity-turned murder weapon.

She keeps reading until her hand grows limp and her eyes close. The book falls to the bed. I stand up and walk to her. I fold the blanket in half and hold it up towards her head, knowing I'll have to pin her down so she can't escape. Right when I position the blanket where I want it, Emma rolls over, her arm almost hitting me, her mouth turning away from me. I sigh and look at her, hoping she'll turn back to me soon so this can end.

As we sit there in a battle Emma is unaware of, I listen to the noises her body makes. When I hear her breath wheeze from her chest, I am sure she isn't faking. Her mouth is wide open. She looks helpless. I walk around to my side of the bed, lay down, drag her body under my arms and cover us both up with my poorly made blanket. Her sleeping body settles into mine.

An hour later she wakes up and turns around to look at me in our bed, her pale face expectant. "I think I can finally eat something."

"I can make you some soup before I go to work?" Emma sits halfway up in bed, letting the cover fall to reveal her green flannel pajamas.

"Why don't you just call out?"

"What?"

"It's not like we need the money. My firm gives me paid sick days."

"I can't miss work today. We have an all-staff meeting."

"I doubt your meeting at Rite Aid is more important than me. Do you have some life-or-death tampon shipments coming in?"

"I'll make you soup before I go. Chicken noodle?" I don't give her time to tell me she doesn't like chicken noodle soup and would rather eat lentil soup.

In the kitchen I cook a can of soup on the stove. At the last minute I decide to add some tomatoes in. I can't let her get better. When it's done, I rush it up the stairs, soup sloshing out of the sides of the ceramic blue bowl onto the carpet as I go. I slam the soup down on the bedside table. Emma tries to say something to me, but I am out of the room before she can. I leave the spilled soup to be soaked up by the carpet and go to work.

As soon as I clock in, I go to Madison's register.

"I need to talk to you in my office." I lead her into the manager's office. As soon as she closes the door, I pull her into me.

We kiss pressed up against the bulletin board on the back wall of my office listing the employee safety protocol. I barely hear my office door squeak open when my boss, Rick, comes in. Moments too late, I push Madison off me.

As I turn in my name tag and leave work for the last time, I picture Emma gasping for breath alone in our bed, soup spilled over her lap. I wanted that three hours ago, but now I realize I can't survive without her. I run to the bus stop, regretting not taking my car, and hope I make it home in time.

I burst through the front door and call her name. I hop up the stairs and open our bedroom door to see her sitting in our bed, her back propped up by pillows, my laptop whirring in her lap, and the bowl of soup sitting on the bedside table, cold and untouched.

"Emma," I smile and wipe the sweat off my cheeks. "How are you feeling?"

"You fucked your coworker." It isn't a question. My mouth opens but it is impossible to speak.

"I thought you knew," is all I can manage, my voice hitching halfway through.

"How'd you manage to have a shit job and still be awful enough at it to get fired?"

"How'd you find out?"

"She messaged you on Facebook." She turns the computer towards me. "This tab was opened when I turned on your laptop to check my work email."

"It only happened once."

"Is that supposed to make it okay?"

"I love you." I step closer to her.

"Not enough." She closes the laptop.

I glance at her untouched soup, thinking about how I'm supposed to love her, but if she had eaten the soup I made her sickness would've been my doing.

"I've never been enough for you," I say, digging my shoe into the carpet, noticing the dark flecks of dirt it left in the soft white carpet.

"Sometimes I think I deserve someone better than you, but I choose you every day instead." She sneezes then, and I notice the box of tissues on the bedside table is empty.

"Let me get you more Kleenex," I say grabbing the empty box of tissues and the full bowl of soup and leave our room.

"And take your damn shoes off in the house," she says to my back between sneezes.

I dump the soup, watching the cold liquid swirl into the drain. I grab a new box of tissues from the pantry and bring them upstairs to Emma, placing them on top of the now closed laptop.

She doesn't thank me, and I don't expect her to. In silence, I rifle through my drawer for clean underwear and pajamas. I think about showering in our shared bathroom but decide against it, instead going to the half bathroom downstairs and using a washcloth covered in hand soap to scrub down my body, using another hand towel to dry off with. I feel half-clean and a bit sticky as I put my pajamas on.

I lay on the couch, feet dangling off the end, watching *Law & Order* reruns until my eyes burn, falling asleep only to be repeatedly awakened by its loud, steely intro.

At some point in the night, the TV clicks off and I hear a light clink on the coffee table followed by the sound of feet going up the stairs. I open one eye to a steaming cup of tea.

Where Do Skunks Go When They Die?

Making slow strides, I pull myself onto the exam table, trying to avoid the too-long paper gown from crinkling under my thighs. I wait there, shivering, pink bra showing through the thin gown, my face shining with sprayed-on metallic scales because I have a shift at the haunted house as soon as this appointment is over. I am wearing cat-print socks, but my feet are still cold.

After moments like eons of sitting still, breathing in the surgical air of the exam room, Dr. O'Neill knocks once and swings open the door revealing me—small, exposed, and hyperaware of the dark patch of hair on my left leg I missed while shaving. She smiles at me, and I remember she is only ten years older than I am.

"Paloma, I'm not a dermatologist," Dr. O'Neill gestures and laughs at my glowing skin. I don't smile back. I don't want to mess up my makeup.

Dr. O'Neill sits down and pulls up my chart. I try to peer over her shoulder to see what it says about me. The only thing I can make out is my weight and I wish I hadn't. She opens the cabinet above the sink and pulls out a small cup and begins to write a label for it. A pregnancy test.

"There's no way I'm pregnant." Dr. O'Neill has been my doctor since my tumultuous teen years when I kissed my best friend and she outed me to my entire school. She met my ex-girlfriend last year. She knows I can't be pregnant.

"It's protocol for prescribing birth control."

I've been on birth control since I was fourteen years old. If I don't take it, I faint when I get my period. When I was sixteen I decided I didn't need the pills anymore and one day at work—I was a caddy at the country club of the bougie neighborhood across town— I passed out in the middle of the golf course, blood staining my white tennis skirt.

Waiting for Dr. O'Neill to return, I pull out my phone to text my roommate Maggie, who is waiting for me in the car.

Doc's makin me take a pregnancy test. How stupid is that? Will only be a few more mins

After twenty minutes and an obviously negative test, Maggie drives me to the amusement park where I work, complaining about how she should've brought her flashcards to study for her finals while she waited for me.

"When do you get your car back?"

"Whenever I can afford to pay off what I owe on it." I look in the mirror, and fix my makeup.

"Well with all that money you're making as a seasonal zombie mermaid I'm sure you'll get there soon." Her laugh has sharp edges. It is the laugh I have gotten used to after living with her for three years, even more so after I dropped out of graduate school just over a year ago. She drops me off in front of the amusement park and drives off before I can say goodbye. I get to the haunted pirate ship part of the park and Samir, one of the zombie pirates, helps me slip into my mermaid tail, ready for another night of screaming in little girls' faces who think I'm pretty and were hoping for one ally during their horrifying evening.

Samir and I are a great, terrifying duo. I trick customers into a sense of calm with my glittery face and Samir always senses the perfect time to pop out of one of the many trap doors on the boat, fake sword swinging. Tonight, we are electric. I scream in a grown man's face and Samir scares him from behind, making him run towards the exit. Terrifying men is always the most gratifying because of how intensely they resist showing fear. Whenever I make one release a frightful shriek, I imagine them going home to their wives, putting on a charade of how they barely flinched at the horrors of the haunted theme park.

"Can't believe we only have a few weeks left of this season," Samir says in a slow moment. He sighs and sits down on the main deck of the boat,

"What's your next move?" Samir has worked at the haunted house for four years and during the winter he works as a Christmas elf. I auditioned for the role too, but didn't get the part because I wasn't cheerful enough.

"No clue."

"I heard Panera is hiring," he says. "Oh shit, someone's coming." Samir disappears into the boat and I wave and grin at the three teenage girls who walk onto the haunted ship, knowing exactly what is coming for them.

Samir drives me home and when I get there I am greeted by a cloud of foul, eggy air. Maggie is in the kitchen opening a window and using her textbook to fan away the scent.

"Oh my god— do you think we caught Fred?" I ask Maggie who rolls her eyes at me. Fred is the skunk who has been living in our yard for the past three weeks. I saw him one day when I was taking out the trash, his tail looked like a duster as he flashed past me into the bushes. I thought he was cute. I left peanut butter on a plastic spoon in the yard for him. Maggie saw him a few days later while mowing the lawn and called a pest control specialist without even asking me first. I had already named him by then, too.

The next morning Maggie calls Bob, Rid Um's most experienced pest control specialist, and tells him about the smell.

Fifteen minutes later Bob arrives in his minivan, the side of it decorated with a decal of a cartoon skunk trapped in a lasso being swung by an old man in cargo pants. Maggie and I meet Bob halfway to our backdoor.

"What trap is he in?" Bob asks.

"We didn't look in the traps because we were worried if he saw us, he'd spray again," Maggie says.

Bob laughs. "You think he's gonna spray you from the afterlife or something?"

Maggie and I stare at Bob.

"You killed him? What if he had a family?" Bob puts his hands into his cargo pants pockets and shrugs. I really want to lasso Bob and put him into one of his lethal traps. See how he likes it.

"Bob, we'll look on the left side of the house for the skunk if you look on the right," Maggie says, pulling me away from my standoff with a man we've only known for three days.

"Did you know he was gonna kill it?" I ask when Bob is out of earshot.

"I'm sure skunk heaven is lovely," Maggie says peering into the trap set under our kitchen window. It's empty. "Go look at the one under your room."

I hold my breath, walk to my bedroom window, and look in. The trap is clamped onto a small furry critter. Fred. He seems smaller than I remembered. His lifeless hands seem friendly. I want to hold him but stop myself when I think of all the diseases he probably carried.

***

Every night Samir and I take our thirty-minute break together, joined by Frankenstein from the other side of the park who sits on a hay bale and smokes her cheesecake vape. Samir looks almost

167

normal in his zombie pirate costume once he takes off his peg leg. He eats gas station sushi with his gray painted hands.

"Dude, that's gross," Frankenstein says. "Use a fork or something." Samir scowls at her and a piece of rice falls off his chin. I sit on a bale across from Samir where I stretch my legs, grateful to be momentarily free from the mermaid tail. Frankenstein offers me her vape and I turn it down. I tell them the gruesome details of Fred's untimely demise. Neither of them seem as shocked as I am.

"I slept next to a skunk corpse last night and didn't even know it."

"Dude, are you stupid?" Samir says. He finishes his sushi and opens a bag of cheese puffs, shoving three in his mouth at a time. "You called an exterminator and expected them not to kill the skunk?" Crumbs fly out of his mouth and onto his pants.

"He was a pest control specialist."

"And what do you do with pests? You kill them," Samir smacks his cheesy hands together like a clamp. I flinch thinking about Fred's helpless body being smushed in Samir's hands, painting his white stripe orange. "Next time you have a skunk, you better not call anybody if you care so much."

"Yeah and definitely don't name it you freak," Frankenstein says, smirking as she adjusts one of the bolts on the side of her head.

"I thought he was cute. Plus, Maggie is always busy, so he's more of my roommate than she is."

"Fine, let's pour one out to Fred the skunk," Frankenstein says. She opens her vape and dumps the liquid onto the ground.

When I get home from work I take a flower from the vase in the kitchen and leave it on the ground outside of my window. The next morning, I pass out on the way to the bathroom.

Maggie hears the fall and finds me splayed out in the hallway in my worn-out pink bathrobe. She helps me get up and calls my doctor to schedule an emergency appointment. She won't let me change first.

"What should I do?" She asks me the whole drive.

"Nothing. You should've left me there."

I go through the ordeal of ultrasounds, pelvic exams, and bloodwork, all in my ratty robe. Dr. O'Neill tells me one of the cysts on my ovaries ruptured.

"If you keep having cysts rupture like this, it suggests a less than optimal outlook for you having children in the future. Would you like me to refer you to a fertility specialist?"

The thought of having a kid just like me—I pictured it being birthed wearing a fake mermaid tale—seems just short of a nightmare. "I'm good."

"If you ever want to have kids, it's best to see a specialist now. You know you could have a sperm donor—"

"Trust me, I know." My ex-girlfriend had books and pamphlets and years' worth of Google history laying out the options for a future I rejected the two years we dated.

"You need to rest for at least four days. No

scaring little kids. You have to stay home." When I get in the car I tell Maggie what the doctor said. I can tell she feels bad for me when she tells me she'll cover this month's rent.

During my prescribed days of rest, I lay on the couch with a heating pad, swallowing so much Tylenol that I can feel the lining of my stomach eroding. I bleed so much that I go through two boxes of pads. Frankenstein brings me homemade cookies and stories from work, including one where Samir gets punched by a customer who he scared a little too much. I have never seen her without her wig on. Her hair is long and straight, and her freckled skin is smoother than I imagined. She always smells like honey. She watches half of Twilight with me before telling me I have bad taste.

"Hurry up and get better so I don't have to deal with those idiots alone," she says, taking a cookie as she leaves.

I'm not feeling completely cured, but I force myself to make it to the last day of work on Halloween so I can get paid time and a half. I tell everyone in my sickly, internally bleeding state, I was able to convince Maggie to host a funeral for Fred with me this weekend.

"I'm not going to your squirrel funeral. It's halloweekend," Samir says.

"It's a skunk," Frankenstein says. "Aren't you coming to my Halloween party, Paloma?"

"Of course. We say goodbye to Fred during the day and then party all night."

"You're the weirdest person I've ever met,"

Frankenstein says, but she is smiling, cracking her dull green face paint.

For Fred's funeral, I tape a picture I drew of a skunk on an index card and hang it under my bedroom window, right above where Bob's trap ripped the life out of his tiny body. Maggie gives me a small bouquet of almost wilted flowers, then goes to her room to study. Frankenstein and Samir stand awkwardly around Fred's shrine. Frankenstein brought a handful of dandelions tied together with a piece of grass. She places them next to Maggie's crumpled roses.

"What are we supposed to do at a skunk funeral?" Samir sighs.

"Is there a priest here?" Frankenstein asks.

"Fred was agnostic," I say.

"What do agnostics do at their funerals?" Samir says.

"I think it's the same thing, just without all of the praying," Frankenstein says.

At every funeral I've attended, there's always been praying. Even at my abuela's funeral where I played her favorite song, Chelsea Morning, on the flute. I played the flute then we all prayed and cried and sent her off to heaven.

"I don't know where Fred goes next. I don't even know where his body is." We each go around and touch the spot on the ground where Fred got killed and say goodbye. Samir huffs it under his breath. I'm not sure how to end a skunk funeral. Especially one with no corpse. I go inside and rummage through our fridge until I find a mostly full bottle of Barefoot white moscato. I bring it outside along with three mugs and pour everyone a glass.

After the funeral, we all pile into Frankenstein's car. On the way we stop at a party store and pick up several cases of beer, White Claws, and Samir even springs for some cheap vodka. The party is strictly costume free, because we have been wearing Halloween costumes every day for the past month and a half. I am wearing skin tight jeans but still feel freer than I ever did in my mermaid tail. I try not to think about Fred. Maggie won't give me Bob's number to call and ask where his body is.

Frankenstein lives in the dingy part of downtown in a small one bedroom above a sandwich shop called Loafers. Her apartment smells like burnt bread. The ceilings are lined with purple LED lights. When we get into the apartment Frankenstein takes our coats to her bedroom and comes out with a speaker that flashes colorful lights around the room. This is all the decoration Frankenstein needs to satisfy the thirty drunk haunted house employees on their way over for the party.

Frankenstein's apartment is packed wall to wall by 10 PM and I seem to know most of the people in attendance, but it is hard to recognize some of them when they don't have peg legs or gashes in their faces or three-foot stilts. Samir and I do three shots of vodka one after the other, and it isn't long until my limbs feel warm. We move on to White Claws and the more we drink the more Samir leans on my shoulder.

"Hey, hey can I tell you something," he says to me,

his face so close I can smell the vodka on his breath. I nod and the room tilts. "She threw this party so she could spend time with you outside of work." He burps in my face. "Don't tell her I told you though, she's scary." Samir saunters away to flirt with a guy I don't recognize, probably one of the stilt-walkers.

I almost call him back to ask who he meant, but even three shots and two white claws deep I know he is talking about Frankenstein. I have hardly seen her since the party started, she keeps getting pulled aside by people greeting her and thanking her for the invitation. I see her across the room looking bored talking to one of the managers, Todd, who I am surprised to see because he is usually annoying at work. I make my way over to them.

"Hi Paloma," Todd says as I approach, seeing me before Frankenstein does. I instinctively hide my can behind my back. "I'm not your manager anymore, at least not until next year. You don't have to hide that from me," he laughs.

Next year. I don't imagine myself working for the haunted house when I'm 25. But then again, I can't really imagine what tomorrow will look like post this zombie-mermaid-lifestyle.

"I've been looking for you," Frankenstein turns to me, putting a hand on my shoulder, creating a wall between me and Todd. Todd stands there smiling for a moment before he realizes their conversation is over, and he leaves to find some other former employee to make uncomfortable. She has more pep than usual. I wonder how many shots she's had.

"Have you had enough to drink? Do you want

some of my drink? You can't even taste the alcohol."
She holds her cup up to my lips. I take a sip. It tastes
like rubbing alcohol and lemon juice.

"That's horrible," I say.

"Want to dance?" she asks. I shrug and nod. We
head towards the sweaty mass of bodies in the middle
of the apartment moving off-beat to some pop song I
haven't heard before. Sometimes at parties, I imagine
what everybody would look like if the lights were on
and there was no music. Just flailing their bodies to
no sound, exposed by flickering fluorescents.

Frankenstein and I join in the flailing of our
bodies to sound and I take her drink from her hand
and down some more. The more I drink the closer
I get to her. With each song I get drunker, pretend
to know more of the words, and Frankenstein gets
closer and soon we are kissing, her mouth hot and
sticky, her hands in my frizzy hair. As she pulls away
and smiles at me, I realize I don't know her name.

"I need another drink," I say and flee to the
kitchen where I take another shot and feel like I am
going to throw up. I have no way of getting home. I
pull up my phone and start looking for Ubers, but
they're all over fifty dollars. I text Maggie.

*Screwed up at party. Am drunk as shit. Come get me
plzzzzzzz.*

*Get someone else to do it. I am at the library.
Priorities.*

Boooooooooooooooooooooooooooo!!!!!

Frankenstein finds me in the kitchen. Before I
can say anything, she is kissing me again. It's sloppy.
She's more drunk.

"You're drunk," I state the obvious. Even though I am also drunk, maybe more drunk than her. I lost count of how much I've had. "Maybe you need some water."

"Maybe you need some water, buddy." She pokes my nose, giggling. She tries to kiss me again, but I turn my face away. But I can feel the vodka pooling in my brain, dampening my judgment, and soon I am kissing her again. We spend the rest of the party near each other. Frankenstein keeps her arm around me the entire night and I almost forget I don't know her name. We feel natural, like we are it.

The party starts dying down around midnight and by 1:30 Samir, Frankenstein, and I are sitting on the floor eating the forty dollars' worth of pizza we had just gotten delivered. Frankenstein still has her arm around me.

"So, I see you and Riley really hit it off tonight," Samir says to me.

"Who?" I say with my mouth still full of a massive bite of a cheese slice, sauce smeared on the side of my face.

Samir laughs. "Yeah, like you don't know who Riley is," he says. I laugh and glance at Riley, hoping she can't tell I had no clue of her name. But she laughs too, and I know none of them will figure out what I hadn't known.

Then she looks at me and smiles. Really smiles, like I am someone worth smiling at. Everything she likes about me is probably a misconception too, and suddenly, I am crying. I drop my pizza on the floor. Sauce and cheese ooze onto the carpet. I try to clean my mess. I pick up chunks of cheese from the carpet with shaking hands but bits of sauce and oil sink into the beige fibers. I try rubbing out the stain with my shirt sleeve but Riley grabs my hand, pulls it away from the stain as it grows and sets and grows and sets.

"Paloma, what's going on?"

She and Samir are still, as if one wrong breath will shatter my bones. I imagine Riley, sorting through pamphlets and making spreadsheets detailing our futures in charts and I can feel my throat burning as some of the alcohol I consumed starts making its way back up. Part of me thinks maybe I would let her color code my life for me. Samir walks to the kitchen and brings back a glass of water, forcing it into my free hand.

"Fred probably had so many plans. And now he's dead." I say, following my statement up with large gulps of water. I cry harder and everyone stays silent around me. "I'm going home."

"Spend the night. You shouldn't go home like this," Riley says and squeezes my hand tighter. She tries to pull me closer to her, but I push her away.

"I don't want to stay here." I say. Samir walks towards the bathroom, attempting to escape without anyone noticing his disappearance.

"Tell me what I can do," Riley says, wiping a tear from my cheek. It is hard not to lean into the affection.

"We hardly know each other. I didn't even know your name until ten minutes ago." I feel her pull away from me. She looks at me and her face contorts into a mixture of concern and disappointment.

I leave her apartment and head down the four flights of stairs and out onto the cold, dark street. I stumble home through the dark alley behind her apartment complex.

I think about texting Maggie, telling her it's a real emergency. She is probably still awake. She would pack up her flashcards and ten-pound textbooks and come for me in an emergency. I think her exam is soon. But I don't remember when it is. I put my phone in my pocket and continue to walk. I'm not sure of the way home. I continue onward, the soles of my converse sticking to the dirty pavement.

The Spottiest Leaves

I spent all my life in awe of the way sunlight glinted across pothos leaves. Delighted by the way the string of pearls hanging on the ceiling often grew long enough to touch the tips of tall people's noses. Amazed how much life was contained in one room—even when the butterflies, bees, and flies we often received as visitors at Gloria's Greenhouse were nowhere to be found.

Every Saturday morning, my Abuela would rock me out of bed before the sun rose, taking me with her to help pot and water and fertilize dozens of plants. I'd follow her around the shop, tie-dye Crocs squelching on the ground as she greeted each plant with a warm 'good morning' and the appropriate amount of water.

As I grew, the plants grew alongside me. Abuela measured my growth with chalk marks on the wall, alongside chalk marks for her favorite peace lily, growing each year until she sold it to her neighbor, who kept it in his living room and let us visit it from time to time.

Even when I became a sullen teenager, I never tired of my weekends surrounded in green cascades and cold sprinkler mist. I'd follow Abuela around the shop, taking notes in a sparkly green notebook. I adopted a few plants of my own. A succulent and pothos stayed perched on my windowsill. Even when I was sad, they'd flourish, providing an evergreen burst of life to my bedroom.

When I came out to my abuela and she didn't take it well at first, my pothos grew three new leaves. When my girlfriend broke up with me two weeks before prom, I could've sworn my succulent glowed. When I fought with my parents about going to college in favor of sticking around to help Abuela run the shop, the plants were there for me. They followed me to my new shoebox apartment when I moved out of my parents' house after upsetting them with my choice to follow Abuela. My plants, and the plants at the shop were always there for me. No matter how I was feeling or how others were feeling about me, my plants stayed alive for me.

It had only been eight months since Abuela died and handed the shop down to me, and in those eight months I managed to kill all her plants and turn away all her customers. The shop was barren. Strings of pearls touched the ground, not because of how long they'd grown, but instead because of how low their lifeless stems drooped. No matter how often I swept, it was still impossible to avoid the crunch of fallen leaves in every aisle of browning pothos and dried up succulents.

The first time I met Melissa, I had been sitting in the plant shop, watching the rain pitter-patter onto the glass, feeling like a fish in a bowl, doodling on a roll of receipt paper I figured I'd never use. I was considering taking a lunch break—which was just going to the back room to eat half of a peanut butter sandwich on stale bread and one severely expired caramel candy from a jar sitting there since before my grandmother became ill—when the bell hanging from the shop's entrance jingled.

I watched Melissa, who was just a stranger at the time, stroll down rows of wilted plants. She was small and waifish and quiet. Her hair was light brown and stood out in frizzy curls. I thought about saying hello but didn't want her to ask me what happened to all the plants. I wondered what brought her here. I watched the way she interacted with the plants, holding them close to her face, inhaling a deep breath at the base of each one, whispering to them. It reminded me of how Abuela used to treat the plants which made my heart itch. I could only describe the way she walked, the way she held the plants, the way she did everything as warm. I couldn't stop watching her, and it seemed like the plants felt the same way. As she walked past, it seemed like they were leaning in with anticipation.

The clip clap of her slick black shoes echoed throughout the empty greenhouse for twenty minutes before she approached the counter. She carried a pothos in a pink porcelain vase, with sickly yellow-to-brown gradient leaves. I knew reviving it would be next to impossible, it was one of the first ones to go. It started dying a week after my abuela's wake, a stiff formal affair that none of my friends showed up to. An affair where I avoided feeling.

I tried giving it more water, and when it still looked ill, I tried giving it less water. Each day the plant looked weaker, so I did what my grandmother would have done. I played music for the plant: calming folk music, upbeat pop music, melancholic indie music, but nothing worked. I would feel myself getting upset about the plant, wondering if I could manage the shop, and in those moments it often seemed like the plant wanted to get better. In those moments I would put my sadness away to focus on the tiny part of me hopeful I could save this plant and keep the shop the way my abuela would have only for my hope to quickly wilt with the plant. I should've seen it as an omen of what was to come, but at the time I brushed it off as a fluke and kept the plant around, hoping when spring came it would perk up. But now spring had come and gone, and it looked the same. I knew it would devastate Abuela to see what I'd done.

Melissa placed the pothos down on the counter with care.

"How much for this one?" She asked.

"It's looking kind of rough, I can give it to you for a discount," I replied.

"Just because it's struggling doesn't mean it's worth less. How much?"

"Twelve seventy-eight," I said. Melissa handed me a folded twenty-dollar bill. I used my grandmother's ancient calculator to figure out the change.

"Seven dollars and twenty-two cents," I said. When I looked up to hand her the change, I saw she was crying a little. "Are you okay?"

"I'm just so excited to save this guy," she held the plant up high and kissed one of the leaves. "He is going to have a long life ahead of him." It seemed unlikely. I smiled and thanked her as she left, figuring I'd never see her again after she realized there was no way to save my deteriorating plants.

Melissa started coming into the shop every Saturday. She was always friendly and always gave me a progress report on the plants she had bought weeks prior. Meanwhile, I kept trying to make the plants stand up, if only to please my single customer. I followed the old wives' tales my grandmother passed on to me. I cut off chunks of my own hair to bury in the soil. I boiled eggs and used the shells as fertilizer, used the boiled egg water to water the plants and—unfortunately, due to my distaste for them, but necessary because I didn't have money to waste on eggs—ate the boiled eggs for lunch in salads made with browning lettuce I bought on clearance. I couldn't save them.

Abuela had cared about each of her plants like they were her own children. She played music for them and sang along as she tended to each plant, straightening its leaves and rotating their pots. She would let me rotate the pots on the lowest shelves, the ones where I didn't have to stretch my short arms and risk an accident.

"Sometimes I tell them my problems. They're very good listeners. Better than your grandfather," she'd joke and lean into the leaves of a lady palm, whispering words to stay forever between her and the plants.

Without her, the lady palms are turning yellow and brown. "What secrets did she tell you?" I asked it, "and why won't you get better?"

One week, Melissa came in and bought three plants.

"It's my twin sisters' birthday next week, so I'm giving them each a plant. And the third one's for me, obviously," she placed the three dilapidated jade plants on the counter.

"And you really want to give them droopy plants as presents?"

"They love plants. And a challenge."

"Okay, I'm wishing them luck. That'll be thirty-five dollars and eighty-two cents." She handed me four tens and a folded-up piece of paper.

"Keep it all," she said and left with three plants balancing in her arms. I waited until she got in her car and drove away before carefully unfolding the pink slip of paper. In smudged black ink was her number and name.

It took me a while to realize what she wanted—because I didn't think someone as interesting and kind as her would be interested in a miserable failing plant shop owner—so our relationship was clumsy at first. When we kissed our noses bumped into each other and I never knew what to do with my hands. Some weeks we would spend every day together and some weeks I would retreat, leafing through my grandmother's old logs trying to figure out how to bring the shop back to life.

During these weeks, Melissa would bring coffee to the shop and help tend to the plants. They stopped wilting so much, but they still didn't look as good as they did when my grandmother was alive. Every once and a while, a customer would even come in and buy one of the plants Melissa had saved.

"How do you do it?" I asked her one day after an elderly woman came into the shop and bought two of the pothos Melissa had saved from disaster.

"Plants all have different needs, you just gotta figure out what they are." She gestured for me to follow her and went up to a shelf of snake plants that just a week ago looked like someone had sucked the air out of them with a straw but now looked bright and inflated. Melissa began rotating the pots and adding different amounts of water to each one. "See? Shelly needs extra water. I noticed she droops faster than the others.

"Shelley?" I asked.

"Yeah, I named all your plants. I named her after Mary Shelley." She said this like it was normal. I couldn't remember if my grandmother had names for them already. Melissa walked away from me, approaching another plant and whispering to it. I followed.

"Joni and I are having a private conversation, so you should give us some space." She shooed me away.

With new customers coming into the shop, I could relax a bit rather than worrying about keeping it afloat. Because of this, I was having less weeks where Melissa had to come and pull me out of the plant shop's backroom. During these good weeks, Melissa still would come into the shop some afternoons when she finished work. We spent all the time we weren't working together, sometimes alone or sometimes with her younger sisters, going to the movies or watching their soccer games on Saturdays.

I soon learned that Melissa cried at everything. She cried at the anticipation of saving the plant she bought the first day we met, she cried at all movies, even comedies, and she cried when she saw the tiny travel sized Vaseline at CVS because she thought they were "too adorable to even exist." Melissa's openness with crying alarmed me. She had no shame in it. She never tried to hide it, even when we barely knew one another.

One day, Melissa was driving us to the beach and listening to Janis Joplin and she began crying to "Trust Me," singing through tears and swerving a bit too far left for my comfort.

"Why are you crying so hard?" I asked. She cried a lot, but this was unusual even for her.

"Breakup songs make me sad because I think about what would happen if we broke up. I never want to hear this song and think of you Elsy," she said, her words muffled by tears and crying-induced congestion. I thought it was a little funny she would think this way, but I didn't laugh because I knew I'd would make her cry harder.

"Don't worry, I won't let that happen." I said.

"Breakup songs don't make you cry?" she asked.

"I don't cry much." I answered.

"I think crying is good for you," she said. I shrugged. I would never tell Melissa, but I saw it as an unproductive use of time. Crying had never solved anyone's problems.

The next week, I brought Melissa lunch at work but when I got there, they told me she had called in sick. I texted her to see what was wrong and when she didn't answer, I called her.

Three days went by without a word from Melissa, enough to where, for the first time in a long time, I was able to see through the fog of my own sadness long enough to wonder what was wrong. It was hard for me to remember she needed me to take care of her too, as she always seemed capable of everything.

I closed the shop, worried I would lose what small number of customers I had just started getting, and drove to Melissa's house. I stood outside, arms crossed to keep myself warm, for three minutes.

She opened the door just enough for me to see her face, but not far enough to invite me inside.

"Want to talk about it?" I asked, despite not knowing what "it" could possibly be. I realized maybe I didn't know her as well as I thought I did.

"Not really," she said, but opened the door and invited me in anyway. Her house was dark with most of the curtains drawn, but dozens of plants standing tall in bright hues of green made her cavernous home lively.

"How on earth do you manage to keep all of these looking good even though—"I tried avoiding stating the obvious about the state of her home, but I trailed too far into the thought for Melissa to not catch on.

"Even though I'm currently living like a troll?" Her response seemed like it should make me laugh, but her voice lacked all humor. "Once you start to understand plants' needs, they understand yours too," she said as if that was a fact you could learn from a simple Google search.

If she wasn't so sad, I would've asked Melissa if she really believed plants would be capable of putting their needs of survival aside for their owner's feelings. But I also couldn't help but feel offended that even after my grandmother's death, even after everyone left me to run the store on my own, to feel my grief on my own, my plants didn't grow. It was like my plants abandoned me the same way everyone else always seemed to.

Melissa and I spent the afternoon on her couch, folded into one another while watching old cartoons from when we were young. She wouldn't talk much but she said sometimes her world gets dark. The only thing I could do was sit there with her, stroke her hair, and try to make her laugh with my intermittent commentary on the show. She cried some while we watched *Spongebob*. As her tears fell, the plants around us rustled as if they were listening to her problems, ready to offer words of comfort.

We got tired of cartoons and while I cooked her some tortellini soup for dinner, she picked out a movie for us to watch.

"Be prepared to cry," Melissa said.

"I don't cry," I replied.

The movie started as a cheesy romance, the kind of movie I'd roll my eyes at if I hadn't been in a relationship while watching it, but quickly became devastating. My body filled with a sadness so deep it started in my fingertips and made its way to my toes, but I did my usual bit of keeping it crammed inside of me, not letting tears fall down my cheeks like Melissa's were. She kept glancing at me, to see my reaction. She kept asking if I thought it was sad and I kept nodding.

"Pretending you don't feel anything doesn't help anyone," she said. She grabbed my hand and looked at me with gentle eyes, and I didn't know what caused it but soon tears were spilling out of my eyes and the two of us sat there, crying together.

I began to cry at everything, too. Some days, I had Melissa beat. I would cry at abandoned buildings, wondering about the lives once lived inside of them. I would cry at sunsets that went unappreciated. I would cry at happy movies, because for so long I had forgotten how to feel what the characters in the movie felt. I invested in Kleenex, keeping a box in every room of my apartment, my car, and a stockpile of them in the shop.

One morning, I was sitting at the register thirty minutes before opening, and I saw a ladybug sitting on the cash register. I slipped a piece of paper under the ladybug's body, to transport it somewhere else in the shop, where it wasn't in danger of being accidentally crushed by my busy hands or my water bottle if I placed it down without looking, but when I slipped the paper under the bug it rolled over, already dead. I cried as I dumped its tiny body into the trash, wondering how long it had been dead for and how sad it must have been for it to die alone. And then I thought about my grandmother who didn't die alone, but still died and all the love I had for her didn't save her and all the medication the doctors pumped into her to make it so she barely acted like herself didn't work and I cried harder than I had in years, I cried over my grandmother for the first time since her death.

My vision was blurred with persistent tears, so many that I had to delay opening the store. As I cried the thought about the sales I was missing out on lingered in the back of my mind. I heard a rustling sound, like the sound of water touching the shoreline on a beach and it kept going, becoming louder and surrounding me. I wiped the tears, and my eyes were clear long enough to see all of abuela's plants, moments ago half wilted and barely sellable, growing at once. The spottiest leaves turned healthy green, and the shortest stubs of plants stretched to the ceiling. The greenhouse looked like it did when I was a child and would run through the rows of plants, hiding behind ones that stretched taller than me, playing hide-and-go-seek with my grandmother, who still had so much energy for being decades older than I was. I'd weave in and out of the rows of plants, changing my hiding spot dozens of times throughout the game, my squeaky Crocs always giving me away.

"I hear you, Mija. I'm coming for you. I'm going to find you." And no matter how hard I tried to stay hidden from her, she always did.

Téa Franco is a writer based in Indianapolis. She has fiction, poetry, and non-fiction published in *Barrelhouse Magazine, Barren Magazine, Foglifter Press,* and others. She co-edited *Kiss Your Darlings: A Taylor Swift Anthology* and teaches creative writing workshops. She received a travel grant from the Central Indiana Community Foundation to conduct research in Puerto Rico, where her family is from.

ACKNOWLEDGMENTS

This collection, in reality, took me about four years to write but it truly took my entire life to make this happen. I couldn't be the writer I am without the people who shaped me.

First and foremost, thank you to my parents for their lifelong, unwavering support of every dream I've ever had. Because of them, I have the courage to pursue things that once seemed unimaginable.

Thanks to Dustin M. Hoffman, my first and biggest fan. Your mentorship and encouragement were integral to the creation of this work.

To Sam, for keeping my tenses in check and loving me through every late-night editing session.

Endless thanks to Casey, Lily, Emily, Kristin, and Stephanie, for being my family no matter where we are.

Thank you, Ephraim Sommers, for pushing me to be a better poet, and opening my imagination. You made me see language in a new way.

And finally, thank you to all of the women in my family who came before me. Each day, I strive to be your wildest dreams.

I'd also like to acknowledge all of the literary magazines who saw value in my work, and published a handful of the stories from this collection. The following stories were first published in these publications:

"Up Next: I Dye my Hair Blond" in *Barren Magazine*

"The Comfort of It" (originally "La Noche De San Juan") in *Foglifter Press*

"Polycystic Ovary Syndrome Reimagined" in *Barrelhouse Magazine*

"5 Methods of Coming Out to Your Parents" in *Rejection Letters*

"Fiona Apple Joins Our Crochet Club" in *HAD*